THE BOTTOM LINE

A MURDER LEDGER MYSTERY

P. L. HANDLEY

CHAPTER 1

Enfys Bowen slammed her front door and felt the sharp sting of a cold December breeze. Her morning walk was well overdue, and it was the only time of day that allowed her to fully escape the incessant noises of her husband's latest building project.

Mr Bowen had long refused the suggestion of a dedicated workshop, and had opted, instead, to use every corner he could find to dump his materials. His last idea (a model railway that could circumnavigate the house) was one that Mrs Bowen had quashed from the very beginning. But that didn't seem to stop Meilir Bowen from attempting to install a station underneath their staircase.

His wife would much rather spend her time walking a *real* railway line, especially as they lived less than a hundred yards away from one. Her Jack Russell, Madge, was leading the way, as per usual, and didn't seem to mind the layer of frost beneath her paws.

The Pengower Lake Railway had once transported its passengers as far as the seaside towns of the west coast, until the former *Great Western Railway* route was closed in nineteen sixty-five. These days, the modest steam train carried its visitors less than four miles — from the platform at Pengower to the tiny village of Llanlyn. Both stops were on either side of the lake, and the narrow-gauge track ran straight past the field overlooking Enfys Bowen's cottage (meaning she was able to hear that chirpy, little steam locomotive several times a day). In fact, she had heard the train so many times over the course of her life that she could barely even hear it anymore. Her senses were now completely immune to that nostalgic smell of oil and tar, a fragrance that had become synonymous with this passing steam train and its trailing cloud.

On that morning, the withered sleepers were glazed over with a layer of hard ice, and it was a miracle that these old chunks of timber survived each winter. It was hard to believe that this frozen landscape would someday be bathed in the warm summer sun, and the droves of holidaymakers would be getting their first ride to Llanlyn's quaint, little Victorian station.

Enfys struggled to remember the last time she had ridden the train herself. Many would have thought that this preserved form of public transport would have provided the perfect commute into the town of Pengower, but, alas, sometimes a Vauxhall Corsa was just so much quicker. It was sad, Enfys thought, how the locals of this area (herself included) had never truly appreciated what was already on their doorstep. She had often considered her quiet life in the remote cottage quite dull at times. Little had she known it then, but *The Pengower Lake Railway* had a big surprise up its sleeve, a surprise that was anything but dull.

Less than a mile from Enfys' front garden was a small crossing that very few people ever used. The poorly-maintained dirt track ran all the way down from the main road and crossed the railway line through the border of two farms. It was at this exact point that her dog, Madge, was insistent on doing her business. Just like the train, Madge was like clockwork, and her master had the usual pleasure of waiting patiently for her to finish.

It was during this regular occurrence that Enfys spotted something a little out of place. Her eyes were drawn to something bright red on the other side of the railway line. Once Madge had finished her little pit stop, they both crossed over towards a patch of long grass.

Enfys steadied herself for a moment (having almost taken a small tumble on the sharp-edged stones running alongside the track) and straightened herself up, only to be startled by Madge's loud bark. The small dog pulled her master towards the red object, until it was clear that this was in fact a Father Christmas hat.

Lying in the dirt beside it was a lifeless individual with a drooping false white beard and a red outfit. Enfys froze, as if the ice around her feet had crawled up her legs and paralysed the woman from moving.

There was only one person she knew who would don such a costume (and it wasn't the man who snuck down chimneys). Enfys had never seen a dead body before and was surprised how peaceful it looked. She had expected to have been a person who would have screamed blue murder at such a horrible sight, but, instead, she merely went quiet.

How easy it would have been, she thought, to just continue on her walk as if she hadn't seen anything at all. She could have just headed back to the house, popped the kettle on and let the day continue as it always did.

The idea was very tempting, but she could never have forgiven herself. Now she stuck with the grim reality of death and someone other than herself would need to know.

For a split second, she thought the body had moved, until she realised that it was probably just her overactive senses. The man in the grass was a lot paler than usual, and his permanent red nose had gone a dark shade of blue from the cold. His white hair, which was as bushy as his fallen beard, contained a red stain that appeared to originate from the back of his head.

Hefin Charles was Llanlyn Station's resident Santa Clause and, when he wasn't occupying the platform's very own blow-up grotto, could usually be found tinkering away in a pair of unwashed overalls.

Enfys' limbs had started to thaw, and she realised it was soon time to tell the world about her shocking discovery. Christmas was traditionally such a joyful time on *The Pengower Lake Railway*, but it seemed that, this year, things were going to be a little bit different.

CHAPTER 2

The queue for Santa's Grotto was the longest in Llanlyn Station history. Rhiannon stared at the snaking line of children in utter disbelief.

"This can't be happening," she said.

"It's alright," said Alun, who was secretly a little overwhelmed himself. "We can just wait."

"I can't wait *all day*," Rhiannon snapped. "I've got to get him a shepherd's costume before Monday." She pointed to her son, Gwyl.

"Oh, look, it's moving now."

They watched as the line of people shuffled forwards in tiny increments. Rhiannon took a long, deep breath and tried to calm her nerves. She loved Christmas but it did always seem to get the better of her. The looming prospect of spending a lot of time around her close family members probably wasn't helping, and the fact that she had left her Christmas shopping until the very last minute (again) was a big concern.

"It was nice of you to invite me along," said Alun, looking around at the various pop-up stands, all with their generous helpings of festive treats.

"It was all Gwyl's idea," said Rhiannon. "Plus we had to inject some Christmas spirit into you *somehow*."

It was true: Alun had never been very fussed about Christmas. He didn't know whether it was the stress of all those year-end accounting deadlines that dampened his seasonal cheer or the fact that he found the whole occasion quite excessive. His parents had taken a similar stance on the matter, and now that they were no longer around, he had even less reason to celebrate.

"I just don't understand why people get so excited over a meal," he muttered.

"It's not just the *meal*," Rhiannon said. "It's the atmosphere; it's the music and the carols, the mulled wine and mince pies; it's the —" Her arms were flailing around like an inspired renaissance poet, until she saw that familiar, cynical eyebrow rising up across her friend's forehead. "Never mind..."

Alun looked over at the inflatable grotto and saw a corpulent man go running behind it with a trail of cigarette smoke. Judging by the bright red trousers, he assumed that this latecomer was the star of the show himself.

"I mean," he said. "It's just not realistic. There's too many inconsistencies — like what if someone doesn't have a chimney? What about all the licensing agreements with all those toy brands? What about —" He noticed the furious glare coming from his friend. It was a look so blunt that not even Alun could miss it. Rhiannon turned his attention to the little boy standing beside them, and the man cupped his mouth in shock. "Oh! Yes... sorry..."

"You just need to suspend your disbelief for once and get into the spirit of it all. That's why they call it a 'magical' time of year." Rhiannon peered around the people in front of them to see that the grotto entrance was still sealed up. "Come on!" she called out. "What's taking so long?!"

Alun rolled his eyes. So much for that seasonal good cheer, he thought.

His friend's outburst had attracted the attention of a certain station master called Dyfed Simon. The man was small enough to play one of Father Christmas' elves, and he seemed particularly hot and flustered for the manager of such a tiny station.

"I'm so sorry for the wait," he pleaded, scurrying over to his impatient passenger. "There's been a terrible incident on the line, so I'm afraid that Santa's running a little late today."

"I suppose he *is* very busy this time of year," Rhiannon muttered whilst folding up her arms.

"What sort of *incident*?" Alun asked.

His question sent the station master into a nervous tizz. "Oh, it's nothing to be alarmed about." He forced out a jolly smile. "I don't want to dampen this wonderful mood we're all in."

His reluctance to answer the question had now managed to pique the interest of the restless journalist. She knew from experience that any piece of information that was being withheld was usually something interesting.

"Is that why the train's not running?" she asked.

"Mmh?" Dyfed asked in a high pitched-voice, as he tried to act all innocent.

"The train," Rhiannon replied. "Normally, you can take it here from Pengower, but they said it wasn't running."

The station master removed his black cap and gave her a solemn nod. "Aye, and such a shame it is too. We all love seeing those little, young faces as they arrive on our beloved Doris."

"Who's Doris?" Alun whispered to his friend.

"The train," Rhiannon hissed back, as though it were perfectly obvious.

"You drove here then, I take it? asked Dyfed.

No, we swam the length of Pengower Lake, Rhiannon *wanted*

to say, but she held herself back. The man was still trying to change the subject, and she hated when people did that.

The journalist leaned towards him and lowered her voice. "So, what are we talking here, exactly? Leaves on the line? Ice? A small deer, maybe?"

Dyfed burst into laughter. "Oh! Haha! No, nothing like that. Well... not *deers*, anyway. Now I must crack on!"

The man popped on his cap and headed off towards the safety of the grotto.

"Where's Santa?" asked Gwyl, who had grown increasingly restless.

His mother looked down at him with a helpless expression. "He's just..." She glanced over at the grotto. "He's just looking for his reindeer."

"Hopefully it's not the one on the railway line," said Alun with a proud smile. His attempt to lighten the mood was squashed by a sharp elbow to the ribs. Trying not to sound winded, he gave them both an enthusiastic clap. "Hey, I know what we need! Why don't I get us some of those fruity tarts?"

"You mean — mince pies?" asked Rhiannon.

"Mince pies — yes! How does that sound? I'll be right back!"

The accountant scurried off towards the market stalls like a hungry squirrel.

"I don't like mince pies," Gwyl muttered.

His mother placed a hand on her son's shoulder. "I know, Gwyl. I know."

Meanwhile, over at the pastry stand, Alun was facing a very grumpy looking woman in an elf hat. Nerys Haf stared at the twenty-pound note in his hand with sheer contempt. Not even the painted red circles on the woman's cheeks were enough to hide *this* elf's foul mood.

"I can't accept that," she said through her snarling mouth.

The confused accountant studied the note and checked its

authenticity. "Are you sure?" he asked. "It's a bit worn but perfectly genuine."

"I don't have any change," said Nerys.

Alun glanced over at the fifty-pence price tags. Suddenly, his three mince pies felt very precious. "Well, have you got a ten? You can just keep the rest." The woman shook her head. "Do you take card?"

The angry elf glared at him. "Do I look like I *'take card'*?"

After contemplating the idea of paying twenty pounds for a trio of dry-looking pastries, the accountant spotted a small gift shop overlooking the platform. "I'll see if I can break it in there," he muttered.

He had been determined to not let the woman win, but, in some ways, she probably had. The financially-minded man had never been a 'keep the change' sort of person. It wasn't that he was frugal or cheap (at least, he hoped not), but the idea of an incorrect exchange of money filled him with sheer horror. It was the only control he ever had in his life, and he wasn't about to break the rules for some greedy elf. As he had always said: "It's all about maintaining balance". Rhiannon had used another word for it. The name "Scrooge" had been uttered on more than one occasion.

Alun entered the gift shop and felt a slight tingle of nostalgia. He had visited this station before, but it was during a time when he was barely tall enough to reach the counter. His grandfather had always been interested in tinkering with engines, whether it was his old *Triumph* motorcycle or an old campervan that never started. In addition to his private mechanical projects, the former accountant had been quite partial to a steam engine or two, and, during the summers of Alun's childhood, Peter Hughes and his grandson had visited their fair share of steam-powered railways: Llangollen, Ffestiniog, Fairbourne... But there was one operator in particular that would always remain close to the old man's heart and that was the little steam train on his very own doorstep.

The accountant had many fond memories of his late grand-father, and one that would always remain prominent was the afternoon they had ridden *The Pengower Lake Railway*. He couldn't work out whether it had been the rare bout of scorching-hot weather that had made the day so memorable or the fact that he had received his very own green, little steam engine, a toy that had been purchased from that very same gift shop.

The rows of toy engines seemed a lot smaller now than the ones Alun remembered pouring over as a small boy, but they still gave him that same wave of excitement. He picked up one of the transparent boxes and studied the train inside with its intricate, little details before realising he was being watched. In the reflection of the plastic packaging, he could see a woman with a head of curly, white hair.

Lowri Medwyn smiled at the sheepish-looking man approaching her counter.

"I'm looking to get some change," he said, waving his twenty-pound note in the air.

The woman sighed. "Nerys sent you in here, did she?" She opened up her till and tutted. "She should have plenty of change on her."

The ten-pound note began to shrivel up in Alun's hand. "She didn't seem very happy," he muttered.

"Oh, take no notice of her. She's always a big stick-in-the-mud. It's only because she'd rather be hiding away in her kitchen instead of standing outside in the cold. Nerys doesn't trust anyone else to do her job. But Dyfed insisted that she take part this year." Lowri leaned across the counter and almost poked the accountant in his face with her giant reindeer antlers. "I hate it when people don't get into the Christmas spirit, don't you?"

Alun took a step back. "Oh... yes..."

The gift shop worker pointed to the object in his hand. "Are we paying for that as well?" she asked.

"Uh, yes," said Alun, looking down at the toy train.

The woman began typing out some numbers on her till. "It's such a shame people can't ride the train today," she said and gave the man his change. "But it's no wonder they closed the line after what happened."

Alun's ears pricked up like the ones of a curious elf. "You know what happened?"

His question turned the woman into a dizzy bag of nerves. "Oh, it's not my place to say."

The man waited for the inevitable "but". Something told him that this person was very bad at keeping secrets (and very bad at maths, judging by the amount of change in his hand).

"But... it's really quite dreadful." The man opposite her might as well have been checking his watch for the amount of time it took Lowri Medwyn to spill the beans. She checked to make sure that they were alone and lowered her glasses. "You must promise not to tell a soul. It's really none of my business."

Thirty seconds, Alun muttered under his breath. He gave her a reassuring nod.

"Well," she said, "they've only gone and found a body...."

The accountant gulped. It was that horrible feeling again, a sensation that implied he was about to get sucked into a whole lot of trouble. Not another one, he thought.

"I see," he said, as though dead bodies were a regular occurrence in his life.

"Isn't it awful?" Lowri asked, who might as well have been having the whole conversation with herself. "I mean, really — at Christmas of all times!"

"My thoughts exactly. Not at *Christmas*..."

"You know, there are rumours going around the station that

it was found by a dog walker. Oh, that poor person!" Lowri pulled out a tissue and pressed it against her runny nose. After a gentle sob, she snapped straight back into a warm smile.

"Anyway," she said, as if the man had just walked in for the first time. "Will there be anything else?"

Alun emerged from the gift shop with a cautious walk.

"That took a long time," said Rhiannon as he returned. The queue had barely moved, and she had come close to banging on the grotto door. "Where are the mince pies?"

Alun gasped "The mince pies!" He had completely forgotten.

Rhiannon pointed at the small carrier bag in his hand. "What's *that*?"

"Oh," said Alun. He pulled out his recent purchase with a look of sheer pride.

Gwyl's eyes lit up at the sight of a brand new toy train and received it gladly.

"Wow," said Rhiannon, who couldn't help but be impressed. "Where did old Scrooge go?"

The two adults smiled at the sight of the boy's giddy dance.

"Who needs Santa when you've got Alun Hughes." Rhiannon saw that her friend was rather distant, and his mind seemed elsewhere. "Alun? Are you alright? You look like someone just died."

Alun snapped back out of his trail of worried thoughts. "Uh, yes, I'm fine. I think it's just the cold."

He flinched, as Rhiannon pulled off her Christmas hat and forced it across his large head.

CHAPTER 3

Order had always been the key. Without order, there was no balance (and without balance, there was chaos). On a cold Monday morning at work, Alun Hughes was experiencing the full brunt of this chaos.

"Where is it?" he asked himself.

He rummaged again through the packed filing cabinet, sifting through years of paperwork that held so many cherished memories: the hydraulics factory audit, Mrs Keddie's tax return, the bookkeeping at *Barky Cuts*. It really was a Pandora's box of wonders.

But the folder that Alun was searching for was nowhere to be seen. He could have kicked himself. Had he been more disciplined in maintaining the order of his filing system (something he was usually very diligent with), he wouldn't even be in this predicament.

"Are you looking for *this*?" asked a young voice.

The accountant turned around to see his assistant, Ffion, holding up a folder that was about to burst at the seams.

The sight of his missing documents caused the man's heart

rate to decrease back to its normal, steady rhythm. It was just as well too, as the filing cabinet was about to feel the full extent of his wrath (and the last time *that* happened, his toe had been sore for weeks).

"Yes," he said. "Thank you, Ffion."

The young woman handed him the file. "I pulled it out earlier. Thought you'd probably need it to prepare for the *Gallagher & Wastell* audit." She watched him clutch the folder in silence. "Are you alright, Mr Hughes?"

Her boss snapped back to attention. "Yes! Uh, yes, I'm fine. Sorry, there's just... something on my mind this morning, that's all."

Ffion leant against the filing cabinet and took a gulp from her giant, festive tea mug. "Oh, I sympathise completely. It's mad, this time of year, isn't it? So much to do, so much to get ready."

Alun tried to understand but struggled to see how Christmas would be the cause for such madness. In his mind, the whole thing was just a few bank holidays and some inconsistent supermarket opening times. Nothing more.

He was about to feign a nod of agreement, when he noticed the decorations hanging around the ceiling. There was also the miniature Christmas tree over by the printer. Wow, he thought to himself, his mind really *was* preoccupied if he hadn't noticed any of *those* changes.

"Oh," he said. "Those look... nice."

Ffion admired her own handiwork and shrugged. "Ah, it was nothing. Thought I'd get us in the mood a bit."

Alun nodded, although he wasn't quite sure exactly what they were getting in the mood for.

"So what are your plans for Christmas?" she asked.

The question had stumped her employer, but he tried to

answer anyway: "Oh, you know... the usual." The "usual" of course meant a few glasses of *Baileys* in front of the *Countdown* Christmas Special, but he suspected that wasn't what Ffion had in mind. "How about you?"

"The usual for me too: my brother and all his lot for Christmas Eve, the folks for Christmas Day, and, this year, we're going to Neil's parents for Boxing Day — that'll be different."

Ah, yes, Alun thought; the insufferable and obnoxious new boyfriend — the one who kept coming round to the office every lunchtime (with no appointment). Ffion was an excellent accountant, but her choice of men was very questionable.

"Sounds busy," he said.

"Well, you've got to do these things at Christmas, don't you? Which reminds me — are we doing an office Christmas party this year?"

Alun went pale. "A — what?"

"You know, a work party?"

Her boss took a look around the empty office to make sure that there weren't any new employees he hadn't been made aware of. As far as he knew, a "party" usually consisted of more than two people.

"Neil was asking if we were having one," Ffion continued.

I'll bet he did, Alun thought, a dark cloud now hovering above his head. He could imagine that man wanting to jump on the back of a free party.

"We've never had an office party at *Hughes & Sons* before," he said and saw the disappointed face staring back at him. "But I suppose... if you think it's appropriate, we could get some crisps and biscuits in for the last day or something. Or we could both go for a meal?"

Ffion tried to cover up her small chuckle. "I don't mean just the two of us."

"Oh." The accountant wondered who else she could possibly be referring to.

"The office I did my work experience with used to invite their clients. It's quite a good networking opportunity. I think they even got some extra business out of it."

Alun swallowed a large gulp. "You want to invite our — *clients?*" The very thought of socialising with members of his key accounts was enough to bring him out in a horrible rash. It was bad enough that he had to speak with them over the phone (when necessary), let alone try and make conversation over cocktail sausages and cheap wine.

"Could be good for the brand?" Ffion asked, fluttering her eyelashes.

Her boss was even more confused. *Brand? What brand?* Before he could contemplate the gaps of his marketing knowledge any further, he was rescued by the ringing of his landline phone.

"I'd better get that," he said, leaping for the phone and leaving his employee hanging for an answer.

"Hello, *Hughes & Sons Accountancy Services!*"

The man returned to the safety of his desk and held the receiver tight against his ear.

"You'll never guess this one," said a familiar voice on the other end of the line.

Alun sighed. This sort of opening was not usually a good sign. "You've tidied up your desk?" he asked.

Rhiannon's exaggerated laugh groaned out of the phone. "Ha — ha! And I keep thinking you don't have a sense of humour. You should write cracker jokes."

"I wasn't joking."

"You know, Alun, you can be very rude this time of year." She began munching away on some roasted chestnuts. "And for your information — my desk isn't messy — I've just got a particular way of organising things. Not everyone's brain is as strange as yours."

"Is the *Twix* wrapper still there?"

There was a long pause.

"That's what I thought," Alun said.

"Now listen," said Rhiannon, the chestnuts in her mouth crunching away like a bad phone line. "I didn't call you to talk about the cleanliness of my work space." She took a moment to swallow. "You know that issue with the train line over the weekend? Well, someone only went and found a dead body."

"Oh... did they *really*?"

His high-pitched response caused her to pause.

"You already know, don't you?"

The silence said it all.

"I can always tell when you're holding something back, Alun Hughes. Don't forget — you're a terrible liar."

"Come to think of it," he eventually said, squeezing the phone in his hand until his fingers ached, "the gift shop lady *did* mention something about a body."

"You knew when we were at the *station*?!"

Rhiannon's loud screech caused him to pull the phone away from his ear.

"I can't believe you kept it to yourself!" she cried again. Her voice could still be heard despite the added distance of the phone.

"If it makes it any better," said Alun, "it's been playing on my mind ever since."

He waited for the inevitable rant which Rhiannon delivered with conviction: "You're telling me that you *knew* there'd been a dead body sighting — at the very same railway we were visiting — and you didn't tell me?"

"I thought we were there for Gwyl..."

"I know we were there for Gwyl! You think I visit Santa for fun?"

"It wouldn't surprise me..."

"I heard that!"

Alun took a moment to choose his words more carefully. "I just knew you'd want to go and have a look."

"*Have a look?*" Rhiannon asked. "What kind of crazy person do you think I am? You think I'd take my three-year-old son to look at a dead body?"

"No! Of course not." Alun paused to think about it. "You'd probably leave him with me back at the station."

"Alun Hughes!" Her cry caused the man to cover his sore ear. "How ruthless for a story do you think I am? Wait — don't answer that."

Alun closed his eyes and rubbed his forehead. "I just thought we needed a break from all the murders," he eventually said.

"I'm a professional journalist! It's my job to find a good story. And I'd say a murdered Santa impersonator is a blinder!"

The accountant frowned. "A murdered — what?"

"Oh," Rhiannon muttered, "so *now* you're interested?"

Alun sighed. "I just didn't want to get involved this time, that's all. It's not normal, Rhiannon."

"Neither are you!" The line went quiet and, even without seeing her face, Alun could somehow sense a smile forming around his friend's lips. "But you couldn't stop thinking about it, could you?" she asked. "You just said it yourself — it was still playing on your mind." There was another long silence, and she waited for him to contemplate her words. "Face it! You're as addicted to all this as I am. Life's just too boring."

"Boring?" Alun asked. "My life isn't boring —" It was too late. The line had gone dead. "Hello?"

Alun lowered the receiver and remained in a state of sheer

confusion. Surely, she didn't think he was boring, he thought. A boring person didn't drink *Bailey's*.

As he began questioning his entire existence, Alun noticed that Ffion was standing by his desk.

"So," she said with an excited grin. "How about that party?"

CHAPTER 4

Rhiannon slammed the phone down right before Alun could respond. She knew that he was already hooked, even if the man denied it. How could he have kept such an important story to himself? He was more elusive than she gave him credit for, she thought.

The reporter looked down at her cluttered work desk. It looked alright to her, except for the strange object perching on a venti-sized, week-old coffee cup. She picked it up and studied the gift-wrapped item as though it had dropped from the sky.

"Who put this here?" she asked, standing up from her desk and addressing the rest of the office.

Many of her colleagues just shrugged away with their usual, vacant expressions. Her editor-in-chief, Morgan Morris, was standing in the middle of the room, grinning at her like an excited child, and seemed to be the only person who was interested.

"We can't be asking who it's from," he said. "It's a secret!"

His number-one-reporter groaned. "We're not really doing the *Secret Santa*, are we? I thought we weren't bothering this year. I've got enough Christmas shopping to do without adding some novelty item to the list."

"Is that why I've not got mine?" asked a woman over at the water cooler.

"We said we're not doing it, Sandra!" Rhiannon cried out.

Her editor hushed. "Don't go giving it away, Rhiannon!"

"Give *what* away?" asked Sandra, the office's miserable book-keeper. "She didn't get me anything! She can't spoil a present that I haven't had."

"People, people!" Morgan raised his hands and attempted to calm his staff members down. "Come on — it's *Christmas!*" He turned his attention back to the gift in his journalist's hand. "Well? Are you going to open it now — or later?"

"Later," Rhiannon muttered, much to the disappointment of her boss.

"Oh... okay then." Morgan clapped his hands together and turned to the timid young man beside him. "Now, I'd like to introduce you to our new graduate intern."

Rhiannon studied the new employee with a suspicious gaze. Students were looking younger every year, she thought. He was more teenager than adult and came across so shy and fragile that she wanted to prod him with her finger just to see if he would topple over.

"It's a weird time of year to take on a graduate, isn't it?" she asked.

"Actually," said the young man, raising his hand up to catch her attention. "I graduated over a year ago."

Morgan patted his intern on the back, almost knocking the wind out of him. "George, over here, is our fully-qualified photo-journalist." The editor beamed with pride.

"You have a degree in photojournalism?" Rhiannon asked.

"Well," said George with a nervous cough. "It's not technically a *degree*, like. It was a foundation course — in photography, really. But I did pass with a merit grade."

"Wow... good for you."

Morgan ignored his reporter's cynical energy. "And that's exactly why I'm putting you with our star reporter."

Rhiannon went pale. "Excuse me?"

"George will be shadowing you for a little while," the editor continued. "That way he can get some proper action out there on the field."

"*Action*?" Rhiannon asked. "In *Pengower*? There's plenty of sheep, but I wouldn't say there's any action."

Morgan turned to the uncomfortable intern and gave him a wink. "You'll have to get used to Rhiannon's incredible modesty. Don't be fooled, George. You're in safe hands, I can assure you." The editor raised his arms like a scruffy preacher. "And what better way to break in our new blood than a chance to cover the hottest story of the year?" He placed a hand on each of their shoulders, as they waited for him to enlighten them. "The dead Santa on the railway!"

Rhiannon's eyes rolled quicker than a possessed doll. "I was really hoping to cover this one alone. Plus there isn't much to take photographs of."

"You don't need to worry about photographs anymore, Rhiannon." Morgan ruffled the younger man's large head of curly hair. "George has that covered. Don't you, George?" The intern was about to respond but didn't get the chance. "This will be some cracking experience for you, lad. I can picture the head-line now: Santa — Slain! Ha! Get it? Santa — Sleigh!"

Rhiannon could only cringe. "Oh, don't worry. We got it..."

"Right!" Morgan cried with a clap of his hands. "I'd better let you two get more acquainted." The man scurried off towards his office and paused before reaching the doorway to call out: "Oh! I forgot to mention — George also doesn't drive. So if you could pick him up and drop him off, Rhiannon, you'd be a star!"

Ten minutes later, Rhiannon was back behind her desk, squinting at the computer screen. She could feel a constant presence behind her, a gnawing and intrusive stare that burned a hole in the back of her head. Eventually, she turned around to find George innocently sitting there, staring at her. He gave her an awkward smile.

"Are you going to do that all day?" Rhiannon asked.

George turned around just to make sure she was definitely talking to him. "Mmh?" he asked in a high-pitched voice.

"You don't have to sit there all day staring at me, you know?" Her assistant wasn't taking the hint. "When Morgan said *shadow* me, he didn't mean *literally* be my shadow."

"Oh," said George, not knowing where to look. "Sorry."

Rhiannon sighed. "Don't you have some lenses to clean?" The blank expression she received made her want to cry. "Go take some pictures or something. I'm sure there's lots going in the car park."

George nodded and began scrambling in search of his camera.

Rhiannon inhaled a breath of relief and turned back to her computer. She had barely moved her mouse when a bright flash of light caused her to almost fall from her chair.

"What are you doing?!" she roared. George was still sitting behind her, only this time, he had a large DSLR camera in his hands with an enormous lens that could photograph a pride of lions. "It's like having the paparazzi in the office!" She was just about to continue her tirade of abuse when the young man's startled expression caused her to mellow. With the iron cast restraint and patience that only a mother could have, she calmed her nerves and tried to be more sympathetic.

"Look," she said, "you know what would be a huge help?"

The young man perked up and hung on her every word. She pointed towards the kitchen as though it were some exotic destination. "A nice cup of tea..."

George nodded and accepted his mission with the determination of an SAS soldier.

A relieved Rhiannon turned back to her computer and grabbed her mouse. The cursor flew across the screen and opened up a giant online map. She zoomed in on a small lake in the middle of the mountainous terrain. It was a lake that the local woman knew very well, and she found it strange to be looking down on this vast stretch of water like some omniscient higher power.

On one side was her hometown of Pengower and on the other was the little village of Llanlyn. There was the tiny station that she had visited less than twenty-four hours earlier, and the more she zoomed in, the easier it was to make out the tiny outline of the railway line. The cursor travelled along the narrow track at a speed no steam engine could ever hope to achieve, until it paused at a small crossing.

Rhiannon checked her notes; this was indeed the scene of the crime — at least, according to her local source (a relative called Sholto, who lived up on the surrounding hills. Sholto was a lonely man and couldn't have been more happy to hear from his third cousin once removed).

"There you are," Rhiannon muttered, hovering over the patch of grass next to the railway line. Unfortunately, these satellite images were far from being current, and there was no sign of a dead Santa on *this* occasion.

"That's my Uncle Dyl."

The unexpected voice had startled her. She looked over her shoulder to see George holding a mug of tea in his hand whilst staring at the computer screen.

Rhiannon followed his gaze and squinted at the image in front of them. "Where?" she asked.

"There," said George, pointing to a tiny tractor in the middle of a field. It had clearly been summertime at the time this image was captured, and most of the grassland was yellow from the onslaught of bailing season. "That's Uncle Dyl," he said again.

"How on earth do you know that?" asked Rhiannon, before he handed her a mug with a floating tea bag. The woman tried not to shudder.

"Because that's his farm over there."

George was so close that his jaw was almost resting on her shoulder, and he seemed tickled with excitement at the familiar sight.

"How can you tell that?" Rhiannon asked again. "These could be any old fields."

The intern shook his head and pointed to a small row of cottages near the crossing. "That's Trem-Y-Rheilffordd... and over here is the border of Talardd and Deryn Farms. Those two farms don't get along with each other very well, apparently."

"You seem to know the outskirts of Llanlyn like the back of your hand," said the surprised journalist.

George nodded. "I know Llanlyn very well. It's where I live."

Rhiannon almost spat out a mouthful of the worst cup of tea she had ever been offered. "You live in *Llanlyn*?" The man nodded. "I've got to ferry you back and forth to *Llanlyn* every day?"

The intern stared at his shoes very sheepishly. "Not if it's too much trouble. I can always walk if I start early enough."

"Oh, don't be stupid." Rhiannon slurped on her drink in a sulk. "I'm not going to let you walk. No wonder Morgan failed to mention where you live." She caught a whiff of cheap aftershave and realised that George was still right in her personal space whilst trying to look at the screen. "Are you going to do this a lot?"

George turned to see her irritated glare. "Oh, yes. Sorry..." He headed back to his chair and sat there like a scolded puppy.

"You remind me of someone else I know," said Rhiannon, studying his nervous twitching, as he tried to get comfortable.

"Really?" asked George. "Who's that?"

"George Clooney."

The intern seemed flattered. "Really?"

Rhiannon groaned. "Am I really the only person within a hundred-mile radius with a sense of humour?" She saw him pondering her question with great sincerity. "You don't need to answer that."

They both turned their attention back to the satellite images still glaring on the computer screen.

"So you know this neck of the woods quite well, then?" Rhiannon asked.

George nodded. "There's no woods around there, though. It's more fields and hills."

"I'm sorry, did you say you had a university degree?" Her question had perplexed him again. "Never mind. Don't worry about it."

"Is that where they found him?" George asked.

They both stared at the railway crossing which had been carefully centred in the middle of the screen.

"You know the guy?" Rhiannon asked.

George scratched his head. "You mean the Santa?"

"Yes, that's right. That's *exactly* what I meant. Do you know Santa?" She shook her head. This intern was not going to last very long, she thought, not if she ended up shaking him to death.

"I knew the man *inside* the Santa costume."

There was a short pause, and, all of a sudden, the journalist's new shadow had acquired her full attention.

"Well," George added, "my mam knows him, anyway. She runs the corner shop."

"There's a corner shop in Llanlyn?" asked Rhiannon.

"Only a little one. We sell bread, milk, *The Daily Mail*... you know, all the essential stuff."

"Essential stuff, right..." It prompted a question in Rhiannon's mind, something she didn't really want to think about: if the people of Llanlyn weren't buying copies of the Merioneth Press, then who was? Again, it was best not to dwell on such things. "So, how do you already know who the body was?"

George smiled. "I think all of Llan probably knows by now. It's all any of the customers were talking about yesterday. News travels fast."

Quicker than the *Merioneth Press'* news, Rhiannon thought. "So you and your parents probably know everyone in that village then?"

"Actually, it's only me and my mam."

"Oh, I see."

George had uttered his last sentence with a small degree of sadness. Even though he barely knew any different, the admission of not having two parents was a discomfort that never really went away. It wasn't the fact that he was particularly embarrassed or sad about not having a father; it was the look of pity from people that seemed to bother him.

For a moment, all of Rhiannon's frustrations about being forced to babysit a new member of the team had dissolved quicker than a melting heart. She thought about her son, Gwyl, and how he too would likely share George's feelings. The only solace was the hope that someday Gwyl might also still be living at home when he was in his early twenties. Secretly, if Rhiannon was to have it her way, they would be together for as long as

Norman Bates stayed with his mother (skeleton or no skeleton — she didn't care).

The journalist continued to look on, as the young man tweaked his camera settings just to pass the time. Eventually, she grabbed her coat and stood up.

"Are you coming, then?" she asked.

George looked up with the apprehension of a field mouse. "Where are we going?"

Rhiannon smiled. "For a little train ride."

CHAPTER 5

The platform just outside of Pengower had never been a particularly exciting place to start a train journey. Unlike the madness of a station like King's Cross, this first stop on *The Pengower Lake Railway* boasted nothing more than a tiny signal box and a disused carriage, as well as a surrounding wall of natural overgrowth and obstructive trees.

Alun looked around at the minimal surroundings and could hear very little other than the wind blowing through the bare branches up above. It was a sad and lonely little spot and certainly not somewhere he would normally find himself passing the time.

"We could always drive, you know?" he asked his fellow traveller.

Rhiannon frowned. "It's definitely coming. I checked the timetable." She took another glance down the line and tapped her foot. "Look, we're not the only ones waiting."

They both turned to see two tourists further down the platform. Both of them were squabbling over a map and did not seem entirely confident at where they were going.

"Also, there's no Santa today," Rhiannon added. "So it'll be a lot quieter."

The accountant squinted towards a figure on the other side of the track. He seemed to be foraging amongst the overgrown hedges and was very poorly camouflaged in his smart clothes.

"What's he doing?" he asked.

Rhiannon shook her head in disapproval. "God knows. Probably trying to photograph some swallows or something."

"Swallows won't be around this time of year," said Alun, who was surprised to receive a stern frown.

"You know," said Rhiannon, "I think George and you are going to get along very well."

The sound of a loud whistle made both of them jump.

"I told you!" an excited Rhiannon cried. "I knew it would come."

Alun couldn't help but smile at his friend's enthusiasm at the arrival of a steam engine. Locomotives weren't normally a cause for excitement in the woman's life, and he decided to enjoy watching this bizarre occurrence in all its glory.

"George!" she cried. "George, get over here! The train is coming! The train is coming!!" The accountant let out a short chuckle at the sight of her leaping up and down. "What are you laughing at?"

"Nothing," said Alun.

George fumbled his way out of the bushes and came running towards them.

"George! No! Don't cross the —"

Rhiannon's words of warning were too late, and the photographer went leaping over the train track to get to the platform. Relieved to have made it before the train had arrived, he was surprised at the frosty reception.

"Don't you ever do anything like that again!" Rhiannon snapped at him.

George hung his head in shame.

"The train was nowhere near," Alun muttered in her ear. "He's not a child."

"It was a very dangerous thing to do," said Rhiannon, directing her words back at the intern. "Imagine if he'd have tripped. What then? I can't go losing my intern in a steam train accident. It's my responsibility to keep him safe."

"Sorry," said George. "It won't happen again."

"You don't need to apologise," said Alun.

"Excuse me?" Rhiannon snapped again. "Get your own intern! He's mine!"

This time it was George's turn to smirk.

"Are you alright?" Alun asked her. "You seem a bit... on edge."

The journalist sighed. "Yes, I'm fine. I just get a bit nervous around trains, that's all."

The two men on either side of her gave each other a pair of curious looks.

"You're afraid of trains?" asked Alun, realising he had mistaken the previous excited reaction for a bout of nervous energy.

"Of course not!" Rhiannon realised that she had shouted, uncontrollably, and tried to keep herself calm. "They just make me nervous."

"In what way?"

"I don't know! The same way you're scared of heights."

"Whoever said I was scared of heights?"

"I've seen you go up my ladder. You're like Jimmy Stewart on a skyscraper."

Alun had thought he had hid his fear quite well, but it seemed nothing got past this shrewd reporter. "Did something train-related happen to you when you were a child?"

"Just because someone has a dislike for something doesn't

mean there has to be this huge, traumatic event. They just creep me out for some reason: the clanking noises, all that steam and oil, the people who operate them... I don't know. It all just gives me the heeby jeebies."

"The heeby jeebies?"

"Yes! The heeby jeebies."

"I can see her point," said George.

Suck-up, Alun thought. He was a smart young man.

"Thank you, George," his fellow journalist muttered.

"My mam once showed me a TV adaptation of *The Signalman* by Charles Dickens," the intern continued. "I was only five, and it scared the living daylights out of me." He looked over at the disused signal box and shuddered. "That creepy music, those weird sound effects... the spectre by the red light... *Ahoy there!*"

"Yes, alright, George!" Rhiannon interrupted, having been chilled to the bone by his memories of the horror classic. "I don't need any more reasons to avoid those things —"

She pointed towards the small steam train chugging its way into view further down the line. Its hollow and emotionless face caused the nervous journalist to gulp, as the clanking of hard steel echoed through her ears.

The locomotive known simply as "Doris" was a lot smaller than Alun had remembered, and its carriages looked barely big enough to hold a small group of children. Both engineers peered out of their cabin like a pair of giants in blue overalls. One was clearly a lot younger than the other, but both seemed to hold their roles in very high regard.

The carriages were all empty, apart from one individual sitting right at the very back of the train. Once the engine had finished pulling up alongside the short platform, the train's only passenger stumbled off to reveal an elderly man with a beard that would make the real Father Christmas jealous. His uniform was a strange mixture of smart and scruffy, as though it had been thrown on in a great hurry, and he wore a pair of circular glasses that didn't seem to quite fit. It soon became apparent that this clumsy fellow was in fact the train's official ticket inspector.

"Looks like *someone's* been at the mulled wine already," said Rhiannon, as she watched the man go running back aboard to grab his hat.

"Maybe it's his first day?" asked Alun.

The frazzled man rushed over to them with an electronic device dangling from his neck.

"Sorry for the delay!" he cried, slipping on his official cap.

"Don't worry about it, Roger," said Rhiannon.

The ticket inspector adjusted his tiny glasses. "Oh! Have we met before?"

The journalist pointed to his metal name tag with the word *Roger* engraved in the centre.

"Ah, yes! Of course! Haha!"

The ticket inspector, seemingly named Roger, cried with laughter and quickly returned to his duty.

"Right," he said. "How many tickets?"

Rhiannon looked at the two men either side of her. "I'd say three by my count."

"Three tickets!" Roger cried. "Right you are!" The trio waited for him to prod away at his thin, rectangular screen. "Oh, this blasted thing... Sorry to keep you."

"Now we know why the train was late," Rhiannon muttered into her friend's ear. Alun gave her an embarrassed *sush* in return.

"Right! I think that's done it. I'm not great with computers. Give me a good-old-fashioned sales book any day."

Alun could not have agreed more. There was nothing quite

like the feeling of a physical paper ledger in your hands. It reminded him of his first years as a junior accountant, when entering a journal adjustment felt like taking *real* action. Nowadays, having made the reluctant move to go digital, he was stuck with punching a keyboard. It was never quite the same.

"Any concessions?" Roger asked them.

"Concessions?"

"Why, yes — any children or senior citizens?"

The trio of adults looked at each other again.

"Nope," said Rhiannon. "I don't think we qualify for any of those."

"Any local discounts?" asked Alun.

"Ah! Yes!" The ticket inspector began prodding away at his touch screen, his big fingers causing it to go haywire. "I think there is a way to do local discounts. I'll need to take some address details."

"Honestly," said Rhiannon, "it's fine. We'll just take the normal ones."

"No, no! We'll get you your discount — right after this wretched thing starts playing ball."

"Are you English?" asked George.

"Let the man concentrate," Rhiannon said. "That thing's going to die at this rate."

"Rhiannon!" Alun cried out in disbelief.

"I'm talking about his ticket-pad-gizmo!"

"Oh..." The accountant went bright red which gave his friend an immense feeling of pleasure.

"Sorry," said Roger, directing his words towards the intern. "Did you ask me a question, young man?"

George cleared his throat and wished he'd never spoken up. "I was just asking if you were English?"

"Who cares!" Rhiannon cried. "This isn't border control.

Although I think going through customs is a lot quicker than buying these tickets."

Alun leaned towards the ticket inspector and lowered his voice. "Sorry, about our friend. She's just a bit nervous."

"I heard that!"

"I didn't mean to be nosey," George said to the ticket inspector. "It's just I've never met an English person before."

The platform went silent.

"What did you just say?" asked Rhiannon.

"An Englishman," said George. "I've never met one."

"I thought you went to college?"

The intern coughed again. "That was all online. I have met English people over video calls, though, if that counts?"

Rhiannon looked as though she was about to let herself be swallowed up by the platform. "Oh, dear Lord, please kill me now. I can't take this anymore."

"I'm also half Scottish, actually," said Roger, who was more than willing to talk about his background. "I think there's a bit of Irish too, but I've never checked up on that. Anyway, you're right, I'm also English — from Cheshire to be precise. So only just across the border."

Rhiannon had listened to enough. "This is all really interesting, but could we please —" She tilted her head in the direction of the train.

"Ah, yes! Of course! My memory isn't quite what it used to be." The inspector was just about to lift up his device to complete the transaction, when his mind became preoccupied again. "In fact, I think that's probably why I got made redundant in the end."

"You were made redundant?" asked Alun, who was ignoring the fact that Rhiannon had now taken a seat on the floor beneath them.

"It was a while ago now," said Roger. "I worked for *British Rail* all my life. Then they had this big software overhaul — I think they called it a 'migration' — and that was the death nail for me. I couldn't keep up with it. I sold tickets for years. Suddenly, it was like I was a child again, learning how to tie up my shoelaces — only now my thumbs had been chopped off!"

Alun scanned the bare platform. "So now you work here?"

"Work? Heaven's — no! This is completely voluntary. I do three days a week. It can be stressful sometimes, as you can see, but we get the job done."

Now it was Rhiannon's turn to observe the quiet platform. It was hardly Waterloo Station, she thought, but stress came to people in very different ways.

"Oh come along, now!" Roger cried, shaking his device like an Etch A Sketch. His cap had been removed again already to expose his mad-scientist hair. "Work with me here."

George had appeared behind the man's shoulder and was studying the screen in search of a diagnosis.

"You're not connected to anything," he said.

The older man scratched his head. His limbs seemed to all be connected to his body, if *that's* what the young man was getting at, he thought. "Bless you, lad. I'm afraid there aren't any power sockets to be found out here. This is nature you're in now. Unless you've got a mile-long extension cable to the nearest house!"

The inspector burst into a fit of laughter and turned to the other two for acknowledgement.

George reached across and began tapping away with the gracefulness of a pianist. "There you go."

Roger's smile was wiped away to reveal a dumbfounded frown. "Oh..." He moved his face closer to the screen and began pressing buttons that he had never seen before. "Very good! Looks like we're cooking on gas."

Rhiannon had already climbed to her feet and was keen to move on.

The ticket inspector smiled at her, as he did when meeting someone for the very first time.

"Now, then," he said. "What tickets can I get you?"

CHAPTER 6

The passengers of the 14.35 to Llanlyn were enjoying their journey more than any of them could have expected. Sitting in their open carriage with a refreshing December breeze in their faces, all three of them admired the view of a location they thought they'd known all too well. There was nothing quite like a short steam train ride to bring a fresh perspective to a place, and *The Pengower Lake Railway* was more than happy to oblige.

"I wish Gwyl wasn't in school," Rhiannon said, as they approached the halfway mark of this lakeside tour. "He would love this."

"Correct me if I'm wrong," said Alun, staring at her from the seat opposite, "but I think his mother might be enjoying this too."

His friend gave him a dismissive shake of her hair into the light breeze, and it reminded the man of an advert for a popular shampoo. "It's alright, I suppose."

They began to slow down, and she looked ahead to see a small platform with a sign that read: Hannerllyn. The train rolled itself to a quiet stop.

"We're stopping already?" asked Rhiannon.

"Time flies when you're having fun," said Alun.

The journalist let out a grunt. "Strange place to have a stop. Hannerllyn is barely a village. I don't think there's even a shop."

She popped her head back inside the carriage and was met with a flash of light. "Argh! You better stop doing that this afternoon!"

George lowered his camera with a disappointed face. "Sorry," he said. "It's just... the light was really good on you both just then. It really captured the moment."

The two friends looked at each other in horror.

"Well, pick a different moment!" Rhiannon cried.

On that note, the party of three emerged from their carriage and took the time to admire a humble lookout point with its very own picnic bench. This secluded spot by the water's edge was so picturesque that it caused the keen photographer to lift up his camera for a quick snapshot.

"We should have brought a picnic," he said. "That table's hardly ever free."

Rhiannon watched her breath hitting the cold air and shuddered. "Are we both in the same season? It's way too cold for a picnic!"

George shrugged. "We used to have picnics all year round when I was growing up. This was one of our favourite spots. Winter picnics are the best."

The journalist just stared at him. "You really are a strange young man." She turned the other way and found Alun rummaging through some stones. "Or maybe I just attract strange people."

"This is a nice one," said the accountant, lifting up a small pebble. His friend shook her head and walked off towards the picnic bench. "What?"

The lake was so calm that it resembled a fragile mirror

stretching out towards the hills. Alun took a seat opposite Rhiannon, who was taking in a deep breath of fresh air. They sat there in silence for a while, soaking up the impressive scenery. "It's been worth it just for this," said the accountant. "Not a bad way to spend a Monday."

Rhiannon could not have agreed more. "Next you'll be telling me it's a bit romantic."

Alun took another glance at their surroundings. "Uh, yes, I suppose it is."

They made eye contact and paused again. Just as the two were deliberating their next sentence, the sound of a camera shutter made them jump.

"George!" Rhiannon cried.

"Sorry," said the intern, lowering the large lens pointed straight in their direction.

The peaceful moment had been broken, and now there were three people at the table.

"It's a shame we have to keep going," said Alun.

"Don't you start wiggling your way out of this now," said Rhiannon. "You know why we're here. Something tells me you enjoy the conclusion more than the investigation."

"That's probably true. I've never liked fieldwork very much. Even in my job."

"There's fieldwork in *accounting*?"

"Oh, yeah! We still have to get our hands dirty from time to time. Once I had to rifle through a load of warehouse records that nobody had touched in years. It was a right mess."

Rhiannon rolled her eyes. "Gosh, do tell. Sounds like you have some proper war stories."

"Well, I can't say too much." Alun had decided to ignore the sarcastic tone and assumed she was secretly dying to hear the details. "A lot of it's confidential, you see."

"Oh, I'll bet," Rhiannon said. "Anyway, you don't need to

worry, Alun Hughes. There's no danger involved with *this* case. Except maybe being run over by a train."

"I wouldn't say that there's not any danger," Alun corrected her. "There's still a murderer on the loose."

"A murderer?"

They both turned to see George's horrified face. For a moment, they had forgotten he was there.

Rhiannon gave the young man a pat on the shoulder. "Calm down, Jimmy Olsen. There's no killers out here. Unless you count that guy —" She pointed to a lone fisherman over in the distance. "Although, unless you're a fish, I'd say you're off the hook." The woman burst our laughing and prodded her friend. "Did you like that? Off the hook! Stick *that* one in your Christmas cracker!"

She waited for her two companions to react, but all she could hear was the splashing of water against the tiny shore. The blank faces continued to stare at her. "Oh, come on, you two!" she cried. "Lighten up a bit! It's just a dead Santa."

For the next few minutes, they were all forced to listen to the peaceful ambience that only nature could provide.

"Could he not have died of natural causes?"

Rhiannon turned to her friend with a curious frown. It was clear his mind had been thinking again, and, fortunately, she had learnt by now that the man's mouth took a while to catch up.

"You mean, the bloke had a few too many mince pies?" Rhiannon asked back.

Now it was Alun's turn to roll his eyes. "I mean, could the man who died not have suffered a heart attack or something? After a brisk walk, perhaps?"

"Sure, maybe." Rhiannon gave him a sincere nod of her head. "If by natural you mean — smashed in the back of the head with a large object."

The accountant let out a small groan. He had hoped for a more natural cause of death: no foul play, no suspicious circumstances and no element of danger.

"Fortunately," Rhiannon continued, "the person who discovered him has a very big mouth. There was definitely something fishy about it."

She was just about to come up with another fishing pun, when George raised his hand as though needing permission to speak.

"Enfys Bowen," he said, much to the surprise of his work colleague. "My mam would agree with the big mouth. She's always in the shop gossiping."

"So you know this Mrs Bowen?" Rhiannon asked.

George nodded. "She lives in one of the Trem-Y-Rheilffordd cottages."

"Interesting..." The journalist climbed to her feet and stretched out her arms. "Well, as much as I've enjoyed this little pit stop, I think it's probably time to move on."

The old steam train was still resting beside the tiny platform. Steam filled the air, as Doris' engineers were busy tinkering. A short whistle signalled the imminent departure, and the three travellers from Pengower were back in their carriage.

"I feel like I've stepped back in time," said a giddy Alun.

"I always knew you were born in the wrong era," said Rhiannon.

"Tickets please!"

The passengers looked at each other with confused faces, as they were approached by a familiar ticket inspector. Roger Plewes secured his wonky glasses. "Can I see your tickets, please?" he asked again.

"You really need to see our tickets? Again? But we've already —" Rhiannon sighed and handed them over. She had given up on trying to make sense of it all.

"Ah, yes," Roger muttered, inspecting the tickets like a shrewd jeweller with a diamond ring. The man nodded his head and issued his stamp of approval. "Have a good journey."

Rhiannon waited for the man to disappear before turning back to her fellow passengers. "What were you saying about stepping back in time?" she asked.

Alun nodded in agreement. He knew exactly what she was implying. "I guess it was just déjà vu..."

CHAPTER 7

Doris continued her journey along Pengower Lake. The humble steam train had travelled this route more times than her drivers, and she puffed out her fumes to leave a trail that was longer than the line of carriages.

George was sticking his head out of the window like a happy Labrador enjoying the wind in his face. Every now and again, he lifted up his camera and fired off the shutter, much to the disapproval of his fellow passenger.

"George!" cried Rhiannon from the safety of her seat. "If you lose an arm doing that, I'm not being held responsible!"

"I'm sure he knows what he's doing," said Alun, who was sitting beside her, trying to keep warm.

Rhiannon folded up her arms. "Don't you go making me the bad cop."

"I don't think there's any doubt who the bad cop is in this partnership."

The accountant received a stern nudge for his rudeness.

"So, you think we're *Miami Vice* now?" asked Rhiannon.

Alun contemplated the thought for a moment. "Probably more like *Dukes of Hazzard*."

"Hey!" cried a voice outside of the carriage. George decided to join the second half of his body and pulled his top-half back inside through the open window. "This is it!"

He turned their attention to the approaching railway crossing, which was nothing more than a dirt track that led down from the main road over in the distance (if you could indeed call a road with barely any room for two cars a "main" anything).

Alun and Rhiannon both leapt up to get a better view, but there was a surprising lack of anything to see, especially for a recent crime scene. Each of the surrounding fields were walled off by thick hedges covered in melting frost, and the only sign of life was a small stream to the right of the crossing. Before any of them could get a proper look at the patch of flattened grass, only a metre away from the railway line, the tiny junction had whizzed past to the rear side of the moving rain.

It wasn't much longer before Doris was chugging her way back inside the safety of her home. Llanlyn Station was a far cry from how it had appeared over the weekend (with not a Santa's grotto in sight). There were no offerings of freshly-heated mulled wine and no excited children on too many complimentary sweets. Instead, there were the remains of shrivelled-up Christmas decorations, many of which had not fared well during the harsh winter night.

"What are you thinking about?" Rhiannon asked once the train had come to a full stop. She had caught her friend's distant stare, something that was a regular occurrence during their time together.

"I'm just working out how long that crossing would take to walk from here," said Alun.

His friend tutted. "I should have known it was maths-related. You're such a dark horse." She stood up and tightened her woolly scarf. "How about we find out?"

Her question was enough to snap Alun straight back out of

his trail of thought, and he turned to her in surprise. "What —
now?"

"No," said Rhiannon. "*Next* Christmas!"

"But — but, we've only just got here."

"It'll only take about fifteen minutes."

"I calculated about thirty."

The journalist loomed over him with a mischievous grin.
"Well, my calculation says fifteen. Only one way to find out."

"Oooh," said George, who seemed more interested in what
was going on outside. "The café's open..."

The other two both turned to him.

"That's a brilliant idea!" cried Alun. "Maybe we should do
the café first. Good thinking, George!"

The intern seemed quite pleased with himself, and his
colleague rolled her eyes.

"We didn't come here for the café," Rhiannon muttered. "It's
hardly *Starbucks*."

But it was too late, Alun was already on the outside of the
carriage and popped his head back inside through the open
window. "Surely we've got time for a quick eggnog latte?"

"Oh, so *now* we're all Chrismassy, are we? One mention of a
quick hike towards a crime scene and you're suddenly like The
Ghost of Christmas Present!"

She watched him take off across the platform with George at
his side.

"Rhiannon!" he called back. "George said there's even a
model railway!"

The journalist feigned an excited grin and gave him the
thumbs up.

The "model railway" had become quite the attraction at
Llanlyn Station. Built within a disused engine room, this tiny
world had become a three-year project that had all started with

a single piece of track and a toy sheep. Since then, the miniature railway had grown to the size of a small garage and was the brainchild of three engineers with a lot of spare time on their hands.

Alun entered the large space with his mouth hanging firmly open. It was a sight that would have completely overwhelmed his younger-self, and even his older-self was just barely holding himself together, wanting nothing more than to rush over and play to his heart's content.

"It's a thing of beauty," he muttered.

George was standing by his side, nodding, with that same awe-inspired expression. "I know, isn't it?"

The attention to detail could not be denied, and when the accountant realised that the small town on the other side of the room was a small-scale version of Pengower, he let out a gasp.

Over near the wooden barrier was a large button with the words ALL ABOARD pained above.

"Go on," said George. "Push it."

Alun looked at the young man as though he had just given him permission to be young again and was perfectly happy to follow the instruction. He walked over and pushed the button with the conviction of a power-hungry dictator. His heart skipped a beat at the sight of a miniature steam train hurling itself into view from behind an artificial hill.

The two spectators leapt onto a narrow wooden walkway, which had been conveniently set up to allow them to follow the chirpy locomotive for the entirety of its journey.

Alun dreaded to think how long that pool of stagnant water had been lying there among the fields of toy farm animals, but, on this occasion, he really didn't care. For once in his life, he was willing to overlook a breeding ground for germs and mould in exchange for the joy of witnessing two tiny boats in the middle of the lake. If only he could have been the same size as all of those miniature people, he thought. He would have been quite happy exploring the tiny local post office, or the tiny church graveyard. Who needed to live in the real world when you could go miniature?

"You know we've literally just been on a train." Rhiannon was standing in the doorway, watching her friend fumbling away on his hands and knees to get a better look at the mini signal box. "A *real* train."

Alun waited for the model to emerge from its dark tunnel and was delighted to hear the whistle. "Yes, but this is a mini one!"

Rhiannon could only shake her head. "Is this what a midlife crisis looks like?"

"Rhiannon!" George cried out. The young man was dangling across the barrier of the walkway, trying to get himself a decent photograph from the perspective of a randomly placed farmer figurine. "There's even a model town hall!"

"I stand corrected," she muttered. "Maybe this is just a general *male* crisis."

"Gwyl would love this!" Alun called out, as he bent over to straighten one of the trees. It was too hard to resist.

"Uh, yes." Rhiannon felt as if he had taken the words right out of her mouth, and, for Alun Hughes, that was not something that happened very often. "He would."

"No touching!" a deep voice boomed throughout the building.

The unexpected sound caused the accountant's hand to jolt, and, in the process, he knocked over a line of cattle. "Oh, I'm sorry!" The man pulled his arm away before noticing that the cows were now scattered across the railway line.

"Noooo!" the stranger's voice called again.

A man in blue overalls came running towards the model. His

arms were flailing in the same manner as a person in a *Godzilla* film, only this time, the crisis was a little smaller.

"Step back!" he cried. "Everyone — step back!"

The three visitors stood aside and let the panicked individual execute his rescue mission with the grace of a giant gorilla. Meanwhile, the small train was flying towards the scene of the accident at a rate that would suit a silent picture farce. As the cows awaited their fate with a surprising lack of movement, a giant hand came rushing in to grab them — just in the nick of time.

Alun and George both let out a sigh of relief, as there would be no collision on that day.

Rhiannon gave the unlikely hero a round of applause, something that only seemed to make the man more infuriated than he already was.

"People — please!" The engineer known as Iestyn removed his flat cap and wiped the sweat from his brow. His thick glasses were steaming up from all the commotion, and the pair of bushy eyebrows located above them seemed to be permanently fixed downwards. "You need to respect the railway."

"Oh, but we do!" Alun called, his hands clasped together, pleading with the man. "We really do!"

The stern engineer let out a cynical grunt. "This is not a toy."

Rhiannon let out a faint noise that usually meant she disagreed. "You could have fooled me," she muttered under her breath."

"We're really sorry, Iestyn," said George, popping the cap back on his lens.

Iestyn squinted at him. "George? Is that you?" He let out another grunt. "I expected better of you, lad."

"Come on, man, it was only a few toy cows!" Rhiannon's outburst had not tamed the man's temper, and he stared at her with the face of a person who took his work very seriously.

"Do you know what could have happened if that train collided with those cows?" he asked.

The journalist shrugged. "Something more interesting, maybe?" She was aware that the engineer was very much on the back foot in this discussion, mainly because she couldn't care less what happened to his precious train. "I mean, it's not like someone was going to die. Although, you can never quite be sure with this railway."

"Madam!" Iestyn cried out. "That comment was very uncalled for. It's far too soon to be making jokes."

Rhiannon looked around at the grave faces. "Oh, come on! You were all thinking it."

Alun decided it was time to diffuse the situation, and, as was always the case in these scenarios, he knew it was up to him. "I'm so sorry for any offence we may have caused you here today. It was certainly not our intention."

"And what exactly *is* your intention?" Iestyn studied the unlikely group with great suspicion. "What is a young couple like yourselves doing loitering around this station with a local lad like George?"

"Wow," said Rhiannon, "your *Trip Advisor* reviews must be outstanding. I'll bet you're great with the tourists."

Before the engineer could realise that the woman was being sarcastic, Alun took his opportunity to step in: "We merely came here to admire the incredible craftsmanship on display."

Iestyn followed his pointed finger towards the model railway and peered over his glasses. Suddenly, this strange man was growing on him.

"It must have taken many hours to build," Alun added.

"Years," Iestyn corrected him. "Three, to be precise. And it wasn't just time that was put into it; it was my blood, sweat and tears."

"You built this?" Alun stared at him like a newfound fan. The man in the overalls might as well have pulled off a rubber mask in a dramatic reveal. He also couldn't help but wonder how a man with such poor eyesight had managed to build something so small in scale but decided that now probably wasn't the time to ask *that* question. Instead, he wanted to drop down on one knee and pay this mighty creator the respect he deserved.

Rhiannon, on the other hand, had grown more interested in the contents of the café next door and had no desire to give the grumpy individual any more of her time.

"This is all very interesting," she said. "But it's probably time we moved on. I think enough cows have been harmed for one day."

"I didn't just build it," said Iestyn, "I designed the damn thing."

"You really built this whole thing yourself?" Alun asked, as he heard the groan coming from his bored friend.

"Well... it would be wrong to claim all of the credit." The engineer pulled off his cap again, but, this time, it was purely out of respect. "Hefin one was the one who initially came up with the idea. But he never could have executed it alone. I *did* do most of the work."

"How modest of you," said Rhiannon, who inadvertently caused the man to blush. She was about to walk away when her brain decided to override the desires of her stomach. "Wait, did you just say Hefin? Hefin Charles?"

Iestyn gave her a solemn nod.

"The man they found lying beside the railway line? He helped you to build this thing?" Rhiannon hadn't intended to ask four questions at once, and, had she not stopped herself, she would have gladly kept going.

"It was more like *me* helping *him*," Iestyn said with a cough. "But, yes, it was that same Hefin Charles."

"I'm so sorry for your loss," George said. The young man had a genuinely sincere tone in his voice. Rhiannon got the impression that the engineer didn't seem too bothered by the passing of his friend, but she didn't want to ruin the condolences.

"It's been very hard for all of us," said Iestyn, lowering his head to look at the floor. "Hefin was a big part of this station."

"Sounds like he was a very busy man," said Rhiannon. "Playing Santa, working on the trains, building toy railways..."

Iestyn tried to ignore the use of the word "toy" and let it go on this occasion. "Yes, well... that was Iestyn for you. He liked to keep busy."

"Was he popular?"

"Depends on who you ask. Clearly not with everyone."

The journalist could see a dark cloud moving above the man's head. "Oh? And what makes you say that?"

Iestyn checked the room to make sure nobody else was listening. "I think it's quite obvious what happened to him. He was a very spritely fellow for his age: fit, healthy, kept very good care of himself... there's no way the man tripped and fell over out there. The whole thing is very suspicious."

"Any ideas on who would want him dead?"

The engineer frowned, which didn't make much difference to his eyebrows. "You ask a lot of questions, young lady."

"This is nothing," Alun whispered to him. "Trust me."

Rhiannon used to hate the use of "young lady", but, these days, she was more flattered than annoyed.

"Let me put it this way," said Iestyn. "Most of the people working on this railway are volunteers. But that doesn't mean everyone has a heart of gold. Spend enough time with some of them and you'll know what I mean."

"Oh, don't worry," said Rhiannon, glaring at him with pure judgement in her eyes. It was a stare that often made people uncomfortable (and the engineer was no exception). "I know exactly what you mean. I can always tell when someone has a mean streak in them."

Even Alun could sense the awkward tension and decided to break it with a simple *clap* of his hands.

"Right!" he cried in his most upbeat of voices. "How about that eggnog cappuccino?"

CHAPTER 8

There was no eggnog (or cappuccino for that matter). It turned out that the selection of hot drinks at the Llanlyn Station café was a very small one indeed. Nerys Haf, the café manager, did not believe in "milky coffee", and she certainly didn't believe in any egg-based festive drinks. If a person wanted coffee, then they would have to make do with *Kenco* original, and that's just the way it was.

"Oooh that's good," said an enthusiastic George with a mouthful of bread. "I love toast with butter."

The two people opposite him didn't quite share his satisfaction, but they nodded anyway.

"Glad one of us is easily pleased," Rhiannon muttered whilst munching on her rich tea biscuit.

Alun caught sight of the café manager staring at him from behind her small counter. It was that same frosty person who he had received the pleasure of meeting on his last visit to the station, and he was beginning to wonder whether she had something against him. The thought was an unpleasant one, especially when he was trying to enjoy the hot beverage she had made for him.

"I never understand why some people go into hospitality," he said.

Rhiannon could see him looking in the direction of the counter. "Oh, dear. Did she not pour your milk in the right way?"

The accountant swallowed his mouthful in shock. "No, no! I don't mean it like that."

"If you're not happy," said Rhiannon. "You should complain."

Alun was getting more flustered by the second. "I've not got a problem with the customer service."

"Well, I have. You can't charge five quid for a slice of plain toast. And don't get me started on the price for a cup of tea. They gave us two cups and a pot with one tea bag — then charged us for two!"

"Let's not make a big deal out of it," said Alun. He could still feel the café manager's cold stare, and it made him shudder.

"Don't make *me* out to be the difficult one," said Rhiannon. "You're the one that said the bread was stale."

The man forced some toast in his mouth. "I find it quite nice like that, actually."

Rhiannon shook her head and continued to stew like her cold tea. "Well, I'll be complaining. Don't you worry about that. People need to know when they're ripping the public off."

Alun had never been one to complain when it came to eating out. For one thing, he didn't see the point. It was often too late by then, and he didn't see the use of upsetting someone who probably didn't care anyway.

"Oh, look!" he announced. "It's that nice lady from the gift shop!"

The woman sitting two tables down with a cup of tea smiled and waved back at him.

"Don't do that," Rhiannon muttered. "She'll think you want her to come and join us."

As the journalist had predicted, Lowri Medwyn picked up her mug and headed over to their table.

"Where's your Christmas spirit, Rhiannon?" Alun whispered.

His friend could not be more infuriated with his mischievous smile. He would pay for that, she had decided.

"Well, fancy seeing *you* back here!" Lowri said. The jolly gift shop worker had no problems making herself comfortable in the spare seat. "It's so nice having someone to talk to around here. It's been like a graveyard here today. If I don't get to talk to someone for more than a couple of hours, I go a bit crazy!" She let out a short, hysterical laugh.

"So I can see," said Rhiannon, mostly under her breath, and she felt a sharp nudge against her leg beneath the table.

"And I see we have a mutual friend," said Lowri, grinning at the young man.

"Hello, Auntie Medwyn," said George with a little wave.

Rhiannon turned to her intern in sheer disgust. "Do you really know *everyone* in this village?"

George contemplated her question for a moment and nodded. "Pretty much, yeah."

"So you're also related?" asked Alun, pointing at the two mutual acquaintances.

"She's not my real auntie," said George. "That's just what a lot of people my age call people around here. Uncle and Auntie."

"You mean, it's what you call the *older* people," said Lowri.

"Wow," said Rhiannon. "And I thought Pengower was small."

"I used to give George over here piano lessons, didn't I George?" Lowri received a shy nod. "You never did practise, though. This man had so much potential. He had the lightest touch on those keys, unlike anyone I've ever taught."

"Sounds about right," said Rhiannon. "I can't imagine Boy Wonder over here banging out a Jerry Lee Lewis tune."

"I preferred Celine Dion," said George. "My mam had her greatest hits down on sheet music."

The journalist could hear the opening bars to "My Heart Will Go On" and tried not to judge. There were some hits that she would quite happily never hear again and that was one of them. It probably didn't help that she had experienced the worst date night in her life during a cinema trip to watch *Titanic*. The very sight of a ship now made the woman sick to her stomach.

"Wait a minute," she said, suddenly, and turned to her keen intern. "If you know everyone in this village, then surely you know Hefin Charles?"

The young man nodded as though it were perfectly obvious. "I knew Hefin, sure."

"And you didn't think to mention this before?"

"You never asked," said George.

The sound of Alun coughing on his drink filled the short silence. He was a brave young man, he thought. The foolishness of youth.

"What I mean is — everybody knew Hefin. Not just me." Even the young man had sensed the dangerous ground on which he was now treading and decided it was time to backpedal.

"It's true," said Lowri. "Hefin was a very recognisable man. You couldn't miss him with that bushy white hair."

"I assume it was the white hair that made him a shoe-in for the Santa gig," said Rhiannon. "Did he always go around dressed like Father Christmas?"

Lowri squinted at her "I'm not quite sure what you mean."

"Well, the man was found dressed in a Santa outfit. You don't exactly pop to the corner shop dressed as jolly-old-Saint Nick."

"He *had* played Santa the day before," said Lowri. "That's

why it was such a mad rush to get a replacement. Not that Hefin was ever replaceable, of course. He will be sorely missed. There aren't many with a spirit like his around here."

She couldn't help but look over towards the café manager, and Alun noticed her glance.

"So how many members of staff are there at this station?" asked Rhiannon.

"Well," said Lowri, gazing around the café. "There's me; Nerys, the café manager; Roger, the conductor."

"Oh, we've met Roger," said Rhiannon. "If he checks my ticket one more time..."

Lowri giggled. "Yes, that sounds like Roger, bless him. Now, who else is there?" She looked over at the three men sitting in the corner having a hot drink. "There's those three: Twm, Reese and Eben."

Her table turned around to get a good look at them. Two of them were in overalls and the third was scruffy but in a traditional uniform.

"Twm and Reese both work on the trains," Lowri continued. "Poor Twm. He's the big, tall one. Not the brightest spark, but he tries hard. Reese is just here to build up his work experience. I think the prison sentence left a big hole in his CV, bless him. Then there's Eben, the signalman. He's usually moaning about something or other. Too much time up there in his signal box, probably. Sometimes, I wonder why he's even here. Perhaps he's just lonely."

Rhiannon listened with great intrigue and wished she could have shared Lowri Medwyn's positive outlook on the world. It seemed that this was a woman who very much saw the good in people (or, at least, she spoke as if she did). Rhiannon, on the other hand, was more of a glass-half-empty sort of person. She often could only see the flaws in people and was fully aware that she had plenty of her own. Unfortunately, her journalism career would not have lasted very long if she had always seen the goodness in the world. Good news rarely sold newspapers.

"We met an engineer over at the model railway," said Alun.

"Ah," said Lowri. "That would have been Iestyn. He can be a bit of a Negative Nellie, but he works hard."

Of course he does, Rhiannon thought. Did this woman not dislike *anyone*?

The door flew open and in walked a frazzled Roger Plewes. The conductor went scurrying around the room, checking underneath each table like a man who had literally lost his marbles.

"Are you alright, Roger?" Lowri asked, as he passed by on his hands and knees.

"My watch!" he cried. "I've left my watch somewhere. Have you seen it?"

The café attendant shook her head. "Have you checked the toilets? It wouldn't be the first time you've left it in there."

The man pulled off his hat and began tugging away at his own hair. "I could have sworn I had it in here only two minutes ago!"

"Have you checked with Nerys?"

They both looked over at the sour face behind the counter.

"She looks a little busy," said the conductor.

"Plewes! Plewes!!"

The entire room turned to see a furious Dyfed Simon standing in the open doorway. "Where is that man?" asked the stern station master. He scanned the entire café, but his train conductor was nowhere to be seen. "We have a meeting arranged for three-thirty — sharp!"

"Have you tried the toilets?" Lowri asked him.

Dyfed let out a noise that resembled a bulldog shaking his floppy cheeks. "That man's timekeeping is absolutely abysmal!"

The station master straightened himself up and stormed back out of the room.

"This place is an absolute madhouse," Rhiannon muttered. "And I've visited a few."

The café punters continued with their drinks, whilst a shaken Roger re-emerged from underneath the table. He was both shaken and elated, as the conductor lifted up a pocket watch. "Found it!" he cried.

"Let me guess," said Lowri. "In your pocket the entire time?"

Roger refused to answer and went running for the door instead.

"So, what's the deal with Captain Manaring?" asked Rhiannon.

Lowri turned to her. It had taken the woman a moment to understand, but then she laughed. "Oh, you mean Dyfed? He's not as scary as he looks. Ex-army, I believe. He likes to run a tight ship around here."

"Is that everyone?" Alun asked.

Lowri thought about it. "Pretty much, yes. Apart from a couple of locals who turn up every now and again. This station means the world to Llanlyn."

"And what kind of person was Hefin Charles?" Rhiannon asked. "Let me guess: salt of the earth?"

"Well," said Lowri, struggling to answer. "Yes, I suppose he was."

The journalist rolled her eyes. "What a surprise..."

"We got along well," Lowri continued. "We had a similar situation, me and him. Both of us were widowed, you see. Something like that can give you a lot in common."

"I'm sorry for your loss," said Alun.

Lowri batted his condolences away with her hand. "Oh, don't be silly. It was a long time ago now."

The table went quiet, and Rhiannon eventually decided to

stand up. "I'll go pay for the drinks." She pointed to Lowri's tea. "That one's on me."

The gift shop assistant seemed very appreciative. Clearly, the staff discount didn't go very far (not in Nerys' cafe, anyway).

"She's such a kind-hearted woman, that one," she said once the younger woman was out of earshot. "A real good egg."

"Uh, yes, I suppose she is." It had been a while since someone had spoken so highly of his polarising friend. Normally, the people they came into contact with were either rattled or offended. Rhiannon had a habit of rubbing people up the wrong way, especially when trying to seek information. But Lowri Medwyn seemed to be quite fond of her.

By the time Rhiannon came back with her receipt, she had a satisfied grin on her face. "Don't worry," she said. "I spoke to the manager about your tea."

"You did — *what*?" Alun asked in complete horror.

"You're the one who said your tea was cold and stewed."

"Yes, but —"

"So, I told her exactly what you think about her service."

Rhiannon grabbed her coat and walked off towards the door. Alun couldn't bear to look back towards the counter. If the café manager had taken a dislike to him before, he was definitely in her bad books now, he thought.

In the hope that he might have just been acting a little paranoid, he quickly turned to check the counter. Nerys Haf had disappeared, and the accountant swallowed himself an enormous gulp.

CHAPTER 9

"I don't trust that woman one bit," said Rhiannon.

"Who?" asked Alun. "The woman from the gift shop? She seems so friendly."

"Exactly. Nobody is *that* friendly. I just don't trust it."

They both stepped out onto the quiet platform. Their train was still steaming away, waiting to take them home again.

Alun scratched his head, as he tried to understand his friend's logic. "If you can't trust someone friendly, then who *can* you trust? Someone who's... unfriendly?"

"You trust no one," said the journalist. "Haven't you learned anything by now?" She checked her watch and looked up at the clear winter sky. "We've still got a couple of hours until the next train back to Pengower. You both ready for a quick stroll?"

The two men on either side of her looked at each other with similar expressions. Neither one of them fancied a stroll, especially on a day this cold. What they didn't realise, however, was that the proposal wasn't really up for discussion.

Rhiannon had already headed off towards the railway line with the assumption that her accomplices would eventually follow (and she was right).

"I just don't understand what was so bad about Auntie Lowri," said Alun, as they headed along the narrow footpath running alongside the track. It was certainly not a route for three people, and soon they were walking single file.

"Oh, don't you start with that *Auntie* thing," said Rhiannon.

"I'm assuming it's intended as a term of endearment."

"Yeah? Well none of my aunties are worthy of *that*."

Alun shrugged. "Well, she seems perfectly nice to me. I wish more people were that friendly."

Luckily for him, Rhiannon had missed the subtle hint. "Thank God they're not. I couldn't cope with that."

The three travellers continued their journey away from Llanlyn Station until all that surrounded them were fields and hills. Pengower Lake was still nowhere to be seen which meant there was still plenty of walking left to do before they reached the crossing.

"That's the twenty-minute mark gone," Alun announced to break the silence.

"Yes, alright," said Rhiannon. "Maybe it's a teeny bit further than we expected."

They both heard a continuous tapping noise and turned to see George, who was merrily stepping his way along the wooden sleepers.

"You're making me very nervous doing that," Rhiannon warned him.

"It's okay," said George. "I've done this since I was little."

"Your mother never warned you about playing on the railway line?"

The intern chuckled. "You'd have to be pretty slow to get hit by Doris."

"Fine. I'm not saving you if that thing *does* come."

She couldn't help but be slightly jealous of his unwavering energy levels. The walk had already taken a heavy toll on her feet, and this young man seemed to actually be enjoying himself. Curse the ignorance of youth, she thought.

Just as Rhiannon was beginning to regret her walking idea, she almost tripped up on a pothole. "Argh! What on earth was that man thinking when he decided to walk this far?"

Alun almost fell victim to the same hole, but his cautious steps enabled him to skip across it like a careless fairy. "How do we know he walked it?"

"How else did he get all the way out here?"

The accountant tried to picture the various ways a man like Hefin Charles could have ended up on the side of a railway line. It wasn't easy to imagine a person walking to their death, especially in such beautiful surroundings. Had he died of a stroke or heart attack then it would have made perfect sense. But to receive a blow to the head when there wasn't much in the way of weapons was an even harder feat.

"Maybe someone dumped the body," he said, as unlikely as it sounded.

"Of all the places to dump a body," said Rhiannon, "why do it right next to a road? The man was dressed in bright red clothes for heaven's sake! All you're missing is a flare gun and a spotlight."

"Well, maybe it was a spur of the moment thing."

"You mean, someone losing their temper to the point they lash out? Yes, I definitely know *that* feeling." She studied the rural landscape and shook her head. "It's a weird place for an argument. Maybe it was a chance encounter — an opportunistic attack from a passing stranger."

The accountant had never liked the theory of chance encounters. It went against everything he believed in. He had no time for chaos theories or irregular acts of freakish accidents. Everything in the world had its proper place, and any form of random disturbances were not welcome. There had to be a perfectly logical reason why Hefin Charles had been found dead that day, but at this moment in time, he was struggling to think of one.

"Statistically, people are more likely to have been killed by someone they know," he eventually said.

"We're going on statistical analysis now?" Rhiannon asked. "How often does a killer persuade their victim to walk thirty minutes to —"

Alun checked his watch. "It's going to be more than thirty minutes at this rate."

The journalist ignored his remark and posed another one of her many questions: "Who willingly walks to their death like that?"

"Someone who knows the person enough that they trust them," replied Alun. "Whoever murdered Hefin Charles, they must have been close to him."

Rhiannon turned to her intern. "What do *you* think?"

George was so surprised, he almost fell off the railway line. "Mmh?"

"You've met Hefin Charles," she continued. "What do *you* think happened to him?"

"Is this a trick question?" asked George.

His colleague sighed. "Do I really make you that paranoid?" That was one question she didn't want him to answer. "Don't worry, you're not in college anymore — there is no test. This is me just being curious about what my work colleague actually thinks."

The intern tried not to look too flattered. "Well," he said. "I didn't know him that well. But he *did* seem like a genuinely nice man."

Rhiannon concealed her disappointment very poorly. She didn't want to hear how *nice* someone was; she wanted the flaws, the gossip — the dirt, for goodness sake. They weren't going to get anywhere hearing about how "nice" the person was. Nobody ever killed anyone for being "nice" (although she had been tempted to make an exception).

"Okay," she said, using every ounce of patience that she could muster up. "I'm sure he was a very nice man. But surely he must have rubbed *some* people up the wrong way."

George racked his brains for a moment. "I once saw Mrs Brydon's little boy having a huge tantrum at the grotto. Something about not being happy with his present."

"Great," said Rhiannon. "Well, I guess that's the case closed, then. The four-year-old did it."

Alun noticed the young man's perplexed expression. "She's just joking," he whispered.

"Oh..." George nodded. "Sorry, that's all I got. Although, he did used to feed the birds near the Myrddin ap Iorwerth statue. Some people thought the bird muck was a nuisance."

"Oh, what a menace!" Rhiannon cried.

"She's joking again," Alun muttered.

"He really was a very kind man," George continued. He looked down at the track he was walking on and followed the sleepers. They got smaller and smaller until they disappeared off into the distance. "It's quite sad to think that this was his last walk. He loved this railway."

"The long walk to death," Alun muttered, not realising he had said it aloud.

"That was very morbid of you," said Rhiannon.

"Oh, sorry. I was just wondering whether he made the walk knowing he was going to die."

"It's like that riddle," said George. Without realising it, the young man had ignited the accountant's soul with just one single word.

"Please don't bring up riddles," said Rhiannon. "It's like waving a banana at the monkey house with this man over here."

"Which riddle?" asked Alun.

Rhiannon groaned. "Oh, here we go... I hope we're there soon. Can't we play I Spy?"

George cleared his throat as though he were about to give a sermon. "There's a man heading towards the middle of a field... when he gets to the middle of the field, he knows he is going to die. How does he know this?"

The other two went quiet for a moment.

"There's a giant hole in the field?" asked Rhiannon.

George shook his head.

"There's a gun in his hand — a bomb! A bomb's going to go off!"

The intern shook his head again.

"Alright," Rhiannon muttered. "What is it, then?"

"I can't tell you," said George.

"Excuse me?"

"It's a riddle. You're never supposed to reveal the answer until someone guesses it."

His colleague scoffed. "Since *when*? Never heard that rule before. Fine! Don't tell me. I don't want to know, anyway."

"Can you repeat it again?" asked Alun.

The young man repeated his riddle word for word.

"I don't like this game anymore," said Rhiannon. "Just tell us the answer."

Alun let out a smile. "Yes, very good," he said.

"What? What's *good*?" Rhiannon frowned. "Don't go pretending you've solved it. The whole thing doesn't make any sense."

"Parachuter," said Alun. "The man's falling from the sky but his parachute won't open. He knows that when he hits the middle of the field he's going to die."

"There's no way that's the answer. Is that the answer?"

George nodded with a grin.

"You said he was walking!" Rhiannon cried.

"I said he was *heading*," said George.

Rhiannon could sense his smugness. "So that's it, then? *That's* the answer? A skydiver with no parachute?" The young man nodded again. "Well, that wasn't very funny."

"It's a riddle," said Alun, "not a joke."

"I don't care," Rhiannon snapped. "I think it's stupid. Next you'll be telling me Hefin Charles fell from the sky."

Alun shrugged. "It's certainly the most plausible explanation at this stage."

They all said very little for a while, and by the time they had reached the crossing, the mood was at an all time low.

"This must be it," said Rhiannon, staring at the narrow dirt track crossing over the railway line. "It's a bit of an anticlimax."

"What were you expecting?" asked Alun.

"I don't know. A landmark of some kind? A nice bench to sit down on, maybe? Or even a café would be nice." She looked around at all the empty fields covered in frost. The edge of Pengower Lake was still another half a mile away, which meant there was little to see other than a lot of farmland and hills. "I guess it really is just a crossing. Nothing special about it."

"There must be a reason it happened here," said Alun. "Maybe he was heading somewhere?"

"Dressed as Santa?" asked Rhiannon. "It's probably more likely he was just drunk. Maybe he fell over and cracked his head open on the track."

"His body was found over there," said George, pointing to the flattened patch of grass several feet away from the line. "Someone would have had to have moved him there afterwards."

"That's a good point," said Alun.

"Yes, thank you for that, George." Rhiannon crouched down and ran her finger along the cold steel. "Okay, maybe he stood up after his fall and then stumbled across to the grass before he collapsed?"

"It's hard to know without seeing the position of his body."

"Well, it's a bit late for that." Rhiannon wandered over to the patch of squashed grass. Any physical remains of police activity were long gone, and the idea of a fully fledged crime scene in these quiet surroundings seemed almost fantastical.

"A lot of this ground has been disturbed," said Alun, pointing towards a large patch of dirt. "It's like someone's been digging. Why would they be digging?"

"If they were trying to bury the body," said Rhiannon. "They did a terrible job of it. Either that, or there's a giant mole on the loose."

George pulled out his camera from the bag hanging around his neck and proceeded to fire off snapshots like they were rounds of machine gun bullets. He attempted to cover as many angles as possible, to the point that it was starting to annoy his colleague.

"Good luck finding a decent picture in this spot," said Rhiannon. "Unless you want to get more of your *National Geographic* action over in those bushes."

"I'm just making sure we've got everything covered," said the intern. It wasn't long before he had turned his enormous lens in the direction of his companions, and it wasn't going down too well.

"Don't point that thing at me!" Rhiannon cried.

George lowered his weapon. "Oh, sorry. I was just capturing the moment."

"The moment? *What* moment?"

"Your first moments entering the crime scene. I like my photos to tell a story. In this one, we get to watch someone putting the pieces together. The viewer can wonder what you might be thinking by just staring at your eyes. The moody landscape mirrors your —"

"Be very careful how you end that sentence," Rhiannon warned him. "Besides, I was actually just thinking about what food I had in the fridge. I need to grab some things on the way home."

A deflated George let out a disappointing sigh. "Maybe I'll find some shots over there," he muttered and headed off towards the bushes.

Rhiannon could not have been more pleased. "Maybe now I've not got a camera in my face, I can actually think properly."

"What are you thinking?" asked Alun.

"I just told you — my shopping list."

"No, I mean, what do you think about this?" The accountant turned her attention back to their surroundings.

"Oh," she said. "I've no idea. It's just a crossing."

"Exactly." Alun looked up at the hills in the far distance. Farms and cottages were dotted around to form tiny specs. "Which is why anything unusual should stand out like a sore thumb."

"Maybe we should ask the sheep if they know anything? They seem to be the only witnesses at the moment." She checked the field beside them. "Not that I can see any of *those* right now. This spot must be too boring even for them."

"Oiii!!"

The loud cry startled all three of them, particularly George, who was right in the process of climbing across a barbed-wire fence.

Parked directly on the railway crossing was a beaten-up *Land Rover* with a furious head sticking out from the driver window. "You know you lot are trespassing?!" the farmer called out.

Alun had a sudden urge to turn and head straight back in

the direction they came. The last thing he wanted to do was upset someone who used heavy-duty machinery for a living.

"How on earth are we trespassing?" Rhiannon cried back. "This is a railway line!"

"And who do you think owns the land around it?" the farmer asked. "If it's not tourists I have to worry about, it's people poking around and causing a scene. I've had enough of you lot disturbing the ground!"

Rhiannon cupped her mouth and yelled: "We're not coppers!"

"Who are you then?"

"I'm a journalist!"

The farmer scoffed. "The press? That's even worse!"

Alun approached his irate friend and attempted to de-escalate the situation. "Maybe we need to stop shouting and have a more civilised conversation."

"*Civilised*?" asked Rhiannon, who had no intention of calming down. "There's no chance of a civilised *anything* with that stupid p —"

"There's no harm in trying," Alun quickly interrupted. "Sometimes people just want to be heard."

"I think we can hear him quite clearly, don't you?"

"George?" the farmer called out. "Is that you?"

The intern stood up, dusting off the branches from his hard fall. He squinted at the man in the *Land Rover*. "Oh, hey, Tecwyn," he said with a wave.

The farmer was taken by surprise and took another look at the two strangers. "Are these vultures bothering you?

The man's words were enough to tip Rhiannon over the edge. "Hey! Who are you calling —"

"Oh, don't worry, Tec," George interjected. "They're with me."

"Oh, aye?" Tecwyn scratched underneath his flat cap and

looked as though he was going to give them all a piece of his mind. Instead, he rubbed his large forehead and sniffed. "Fair enough." The farmer revved up his engine and slipped it into gear. "Just you make sure they keep their noses out of trouble."

George nodded. "Aye, will do."

"Oh, and send me regards to your mam." Tecwyn tipped his hat, ignoring the other two. "Merry Christmas!"

Rhiannon looked on in disbelief, as the Land Rover sped off along the uneven road.

"Merry Christmas!" Alun called out whilst waving. He turned to his friend and had a pleased smile. "You see, I told you he might be reasonable."

The journalist did not share his enthusiasm in the slightest. "Next time," she said "He can have a few extra dents in that Land Rover. Try that for reasonable." She felt a cold shiver and gazed around at the frosty landscape. "I think we might be done here." The railway line near her feet led the way back towards the station and a feeling of disappointment washed over her.

"If only there was someone around who might have seen something out of the ordinary," said Alun.

"No chance of that in this location," said Rhiannon. "There's nobody around for miles. Just grumpy people in Land Rovers. I mean, how are we supposed to figure this thing out if we don't even know the position of the victim's body?"

"We could always ask the person who found him?"

George gave them an innocent shrug, as the adults turned to him.

"You know the person who found Hefin Charles' body?" asked Alun.

The intern smiled. "Of course! Everyone knows everyone in Llanlyn."

CHAPTER 10

Enfys Bowen's cottage had the same exact appearance as all the other cottages on Trem-Y-Rheilffordd, so much so that Rhiannon was surprised how her intern had managed to locate the right one.

After a firm knock against the solid front door, the growls of a suspicious Jack Russell caused them all to jump.

"Down!" cried a muffled voice, and the door swung open to reveal a woman covered from head to toe in flour. Her command had done little to calm the dog down, and the snarling animal continued to show its teeth.

"Sorry to disturb you," said Rhiannon. "Looks like we've caught you in the middle of something."

Enfys dusted off some white powder from her cheek. "In the middle of a disaster, you mean. I knew I should have followed the recipe." She paused and noticed the young man. "Oh, hello, George."

"Hello, Mrs Bowen."

"You look absolutely freezing."

Alun raised his shivering hand. "We all are, actually."

The woman pulled her dog back so that he wasn't still blocking the door. "Oh, get inside — right now!"

The accountant took a step forward across the doormat.

"Not *you*!" Enfys cried. "The dog!"

"Oh," said Alun, and he took a step back again.

"It's okay," said George. "They're not from the police. One of them's my work colleague from the paper."

"The paper?" Enfys jiggled with excitement. "Oh, well — I think you'd better come in."

Rhiannon turned to her apprehensive friend. "She means you now."

Alun took the hint and dashed inside for warmth.

"You'll have to excuse the mess," Enfys said once they had all entered the living room. "My husband is somewhat of a... well, I don't know what he is these days, but he doesn't half cause a mess. Retirement hasn't really suited him."

The visitors couldn't help but notice the railway track snaking around the dining table.

"He builds model trains?" Alun asked.

"Oh," said Enfys. "I wouldn't use that word around *him*. According to my husband, the size makes no difference. And I can assure you it does!"

The woman giggled and gestured for them to take a seat.

"What is it with people and trains?" Rhiannon asked. "I just don't get it."

"Don't get me started," said Enfys. "My other half's only just finished his little miniature railway project and now he's moved on to bigger things."

"*Bigger* things?"

Enfys pointed towards the window overlooking the back garden. "He's now working on a miniature railway that you can ride on. It's taken him years to get round to doing up the garden, and now he's out there everyday."

"Correct me if I'm wrong," said Rhiannon. "But isn't there a train that goes straight past your house?"

Enfys flapped her hands. "You're preaching to the choir over here." She was about to step on a mini engine room in front of the windowsill when she pulled her foot back. "Honestly, I'm beginning to wonder whether there's something wrong with him. The other day he made me wait for that little train to come around to deliver my toast. There were crumbs everywhere!"

"Does the train go all the way into the kitchen?" Alun asked, failing to contain his excitement. The thought of such a thing gave him butterflies.

"It goes all the way around the flaming *house!*" Enfys cried.

The accountant and the junior photographer both let out a deep breath and let it all sink in.

"That's so cool," said George.

"It's certainly *not* cool!" Enfys snapped. "Try living in a house where all the doors have to be left open. I can't even use the bathroom without the risk of a Flying Scotsman interrupting me.

Rhiannon's mouth dropped open in disbelief, as the others tried not to laugh. "You must really love your husband, Mrs Bowen."

Enfys grumbled and headed off to the kitchen to make a round of tea.

"Your husband must be quite inspired by the model railway at the station!" Alun called out.

There was a pause, and Enfys appeared in the doorway with a grave face. "We don't talk about that in this house anymore."

"Oh, I'm sorry."

"It's something of a sore subject after the big fall-out."

"Fall-out?" Rhiannon asked.

Enfys sighed. "Before... all of this —" She pointed at the track running around her living room. "My husband was always over at the station. I quite miss those days, actually. We had a normal house back then."

Alun managed to cast his mind back to that perfect, little world with its carefully arranged people. "So, he was involved in the miniature build?"

"Involved? It was his idea!"

Alun and Rhiannon both looked at each other. It seemed there was more to the creation story than the man they had spoken to had let on.

"We spoke to the engineer today," said the journalist.

Enfys' face soured. "Oh, not that dreadful man. I can't stand him."

"Iestyn?" asked George.

His host rushed over to the window to check for prying ears. "I wouldn't go mentioning that name in this house," she said. "Those two are mortal enemies."

"Over a miniature railway?" asked Rhiannon.

"Wars are often fought over patches of land," said Alun, as though the whole thing was quite reasonable.

"Not land where the cows are less than an inch tall!"

Enfys Bowen shook her head in despair. "They were all such good friends at one point. My husband, Iestyn, Hefin..."

The last name sent a ripple of intrigue across the entire room.

"Hefin Charles?" Rhiannon asked.

"Hefin got caught up in the middle," Enfys continued, "bless him. He was probably the biggest casualty in that whole thing."

"The same Hefin Charles who is now *dead*?"

The journalist's blunt question caused the woman to gasp. "Oh, goodness!" she cried with a sob. "I keep forgetting he's no longer with us. Oh, the poor man!"

Rhiannon waited for her to pull out a tissue and wipe her nose. "I'm confused. First, I thought it was that grumpy engineer who built the model, now you're saying it was *three* people?"

Enfys finished blowing her nose. "It was my husband's vision that started the whole thing. He drew up the original plans and showed them to Iestyn — he was a surveyor, you see. They built the whole thing together, and Hefin chipped in to help. The three of them actually made a good team. Hefin was quite resourceful, Iesyn was a skilled engineer and my husband, well, he had all the enthusiasm to see it through."

"So what went wrong?" asked Alun.

"Well, it was all fun and games until it was finished. Then my husband found out that Iestyn was taking all of the credit for it." Enfys pointed at the journalist. "They even had someone down from your newspaper to cover it."

"Sounds like I dodged a bullet on *that* one," Rhiannon muttered.

"We read the article and that little rat hadn't even mentioned my husband's name! Then he put a lock on the building that only he had the keys for." The woman shuddered. "Meilir was so cross. That's when he made the decision to build his own railway — one where he had full control."

Rhiannon had yet to meet Mr Bowen, but she was already starting to dislike the man. From her perspective, it sounded like there was a whole load of egos involved and not a lot of common sense. "So what was Hefin's opinion on all of this?"

Enfys chose her reply very carefully. "Hefin was... somewhat of a people-pleaser. I don't think he really cared about model railways, but it put him in a very awkward situation when he offered to help my husband."

"That man really was quite the Samaritan," said Rhiannon.

"Oh, yes!" Enfys reached for the tissue again. "He was such a giving man. There was no reason for anyone to dislike him."

"I sense a *but*..."

"Iestyn saw it as taking sides, you see. Like a betrayal. Hefin had made his choice and that was that."

"You make it sound like he crossed the picket line."

"He sort of did in a way. By helping my husband with his new project, he'd made his loyalties quite clear."

The sound of a train whistle made all of the visitors leap out of their chairs. Out of nowhere, a tiny steam train came flying into the room along the web of tracks. Enfys checked her watch and nodded. "Yes," she said. "That sounds about right. It's the fourteen-forty."

Alun and Rhiannon both looked at each other. Just as one of them was about to try and wrap things up, they heard a loud cry coming from outside. Everyone rushed to the window to find a furious Meilir Bowen jumping up and down in the garden. He clutched his sore finger and began cursing at the dismantled engine, lying on the ground.

"I think he's really missing Hefin's help," said Enfys, as her husband continued his outburst by kicking the pile of machinery.

"Well," said Alun, "Hefin Charles is sort of the reason for our visit."

Enfys turned to him in surprise. "Really?" She suddenly remembered about the tea and rushed off towards the kitchen. "I'm so sorry to keep you waiting for your drinks."

"Honestly!" Rhiannon called out. "We don't want to keep *you* much longer!"

"No, no! There's no excuse for bad hospitality!"

The journalist turned to her fellow visitors and signalled towards the open doorway. They all stood up and snuck their way to the kitchen.

"We can't stay for too long," said George.

Rhiannon was about to step forward onto the terracotta tiles, when she heard a growl from a nearby dog bed. She respected the Jack Russell's wishes and moved back to the safety of the doorway.

"I'm aware that it was you who found the body," she said. "That must have been awful."

Enfys kept her attention on the tea-making and began placing a container of scones on a plate. "Yes, it was. But not as dramatic as it sounds." The woman licked some jam from her finger. "I always imagined finding a dead body to be this big scene where someone screams out in horror. But that must be all the sound effects in those TV programmes.

"How do you mean?" asked Rhiannon.

"It was all so quiet," said Enfys, her mind reenacting the moment. "There he was, Hefin Charles, lying beside the railway line. He looked quite peaceful in a way."

"Do you remember what position he was in?"

Enfys tilted up her head towards the ceiling. "Oh, now you're asking me." She scrunched up her eyes and tried to recall. "He was lying there in the grass."

"Facing upwards?" Alun asked.

"Uh, sort of. He was lying on his side, facing me. That's how I recognised his face." She shuddered. "It gives me a chill just thinking about it."

"And was there much blood? Did it look like he'd been struck?"

"Oh, heavens, I don't know. That was the last thing I was thinking about. But there was definitely blood. His hair was usually white and it looked soaked through. His Santa hat was lying in the dirt, and he seemed to be in full costume."

The woman continued making the tea, as her audience looked on from the doorway. Rhiannon was somewhat disappointed. She was beginning to realise that this person was going to provide them with few details that they already knew.

"Did you see anyone else out there at all?" she asked. "Even on your walk there?"

"It was early morning. I didn't see anyone. If there had been another walker, they probably would have found the body first."

Enfys was just about to say something else, when the landline phone beside her burst into life. "That flaming thing," she said, calming her nerves.

"Did you want to get that?" Rhiannon asked.

"There's no point," said Enfys, shaking her head and reaching for some more plates. "It'll only be my neighbour, Mrs Hendry. She calls me every day to moider my ears. Thank God she lives on a mountain."

Rhiannon frowned. "A mountain? I thought you said she was your neighbour."

"Oh, well, I suppose it's more of a hillside than a mountain, but it's pretty high up. She's still a neighbour, though, and the nosiest one you'll ever meet." Enfys could see the perplexed faces, and she pointed to the kitchen window. "Have a look. She's the white farmhouse straight ahead."

The curious journalist headed over to the windowsill and squinted. All she could see was a line of enormous hills in the far distance, which were indeed closer in scale to a mountain than a hill. In the middle was a white spec that became blurred the more she tried to focus. Her eyesight was not what it used to be, she thought. There was a time she could make out the number of a London night bus long before any of her friends. Now she could barely read a billboard without getting a headache.

"You can't be talking about *that* house," she said. "It must be miles away."

"It's close enough that she can see my husband and me leave the house," said Enfys with a snort. "She spends all day by her window with a pair of binoculars, spying on people."

Rhiannon's mind was ticking away. "Does she, really?"

"Only the other day, she called up to say how nice our wreath is. Then she proceeded to insist that my car had a slow puncture and how I should probably get it looked at. That's probably what she's calling about now. Wants to see if I've done it yet. Some people just don't seem to have any social awareness whatsoever." Enfys finished laying out all of the baked goods and took a step back to admire her enormous spread. "Now then," she said. "Do you think that's enough?"

CHAPTER 11

Doris ground to a halt and waited for her passengers to disembark. Alun stepped down onto the single platform as though he had returned home from an epic journey across the Trans-Siberian Railway. He bid his fellow traveller a brief farewell and continued the final leg on foot.

Back at home, there was a friendly face waiting for him at the front door. She leapt up into the air and wagged her furry tail.

"Hello, Peg," he said. "You'll never guess where I've been today." The Border Collie stared at him with those pleading eyes. "Come on, then."

Alun grabbed her lead and soon he was back outside in the cold. The extra mileage was already taking its toll on the accountant's sore feet. Normally, his walks with Peg were his only source of steps in a day, and now he was well on his way to performing a personal best.

If it weren't for his loyal dog, he would hardly be getting in any form of exercise whatsoever. His canine friend provided him with many additional benefits: companionship, unconditional love, security, protection... But her contribution to his cardiovascular system was something he would probably be eternally grateful for.

As the sun had finally set, and the two housemates came wandering along Pengower High Street, Alun was struck by a glimmering display of Christmas lights. These tiny bulbs with their glowing centres all melded together to spread a wave of seasonal cheer towards the residents of this small town. Even the most un-Christmassy resident of all couldn't help but be surprised by their hypnotic beauty. They were a well-needed beacon of warmth during a dark and unforgiving time of year.

Many of the shops were still open and most of their windows were stuffed with decorations that only ever saw the light of day for one month a year. It had occurred to Alun, as he watched the shoppers dash from shop to shop, that his need for buying Christmas gifts had slowly dwindled over the years. With his parents gone and his long-term girlfriend a distant memory, there was no longer anyone left that he really needed to buy for. He could quite easily have not bought anything at all that year, he thought to himself, and nobody would have been any the wiser. If he had been happy to settle for a microwave meal for Christmas Day, he would have saved a fortune.

It was during that moment, as he caught his reflection in the shop window of a local jeweller, that he was overwhelmed with a strange feeling of emptiness. Perhaps he really was a modern day Scrooge, he thought. If he remembered the story rightly, Ebeneezer was quite partial to saving a bob or two, making do with a cold home and a plate of bread and cheese for his supper. All that was setting the accountant apart at this stage was the absence of a dead fireplace (and that was only because he didn't have one). But he had been keeping his central heating running at a bare minimum this year and was determined not to let the utility companies win.

Something had to change, he thought. If he didn't take some

kind of action soon, he would end up like that Dickensian businessman, floating around the sky on Christmas Eve, talking to spirits whilst dressed in his pyjamas (and nobody wanted that). He would much rather be remembered as a caring and generous individual — someone like Hefin Charles (without the *death by the side of a railway line* bit, of course). "Alun!"

The voice had startled the accountant, as he realised he was staring aimlessly at a display of diamond rings. He turned to find Ffion standing in the shop doorway with a bag of shopping in each hand.

"Oh," he said. "Hello."

"You remember Alun?" she asked the man beside her, who was also clutching two bags of shopping.

The boyfriend stared at him. "Oh, yeah... I know the face."

Alun squeezed the dog lead in his hand. The man should have remembered him by now, he thought. He only came round his office every lunchtime to use their facilities. He'd only spoken to him *several* times.

"I know Neil," Alun muttered.

Neil turned to his girlfriend. "Course, babe. I know who —"

"Alun," the accountant added. "The name's Alun."

"Yeah, I know," the other man said, defensively.

Ffion noticed that her boss was facing a shop window full of jewellery. "Oooooh! Someone's a lucky person. Doing a bit of Christmas shopping, then, are we?"

"Uh, yes. Something like that."

The young woman jumped to his side and studied the display. "Go on, then. Which one you got your eye on?"

Despite the cold conditions, Alun began to suddenly feel rather hot and flustered. "Oh, I don't really —"

"You know what the stuff you got to watch out for is," said Neil, barging himself in between them.

"Here we go," said Ffion with a groan. "Think you're an expert do you?"

Her boyfriend gave her a playful wink. "It's all about the surface roughness."

"The what?"

"The smoothness, babe." The man began caressing his girl-friend's cheek, a move that caused a sudden bout of nausea for the accountant. Even Peg seemed repulsed. "If the diamond's too rough, it loses its value."

"They all look the same to me," Alun muttered.

Neil placed a hand on his shoulder and pulled him in. "Aye, but that's why you need a keen eye like mine, you see." He pointed at a necklace dangling from a severed mannequin. "That one! You see how smooth it looks? That's proper quality, mate."

"I'm sure Alun isn't looking to spend *that* much," said Ffion.

"How do you know?" asked Neil. "He's a proper high-flyer, this bloke."

Alun did not appreciate the pat on the back, whatsoever.

"You're forgetting who helps with his books," Ffion added.

Her boss had heard enough. "Actually, I'm thinking of taking it," he announced.

The couple looked at each other in surprise.

"Are you sure, Alun?" his junior accountant asked. "It's quite a lot."

"There should be no expense spared when it comes to Christmas," Alun replied.

Neil clapped his hands together with excitement. "I can't wait for this work party, then!"

The accountant grimaced. He had forgotten about the party.

"Well," said Neil, gesturing to the shop doorway. "Off you go, then!"

Alun stared at the price tag again. "I might just look at a few more before I go in. Don't let me keep you both."

"It's no dogs allowed," said Ffion. "Do you want us to watch her whilst you're inside?"

Peg shook her tail and, for a split second, her owner could have sworn she was laughing at him.

"Oh, no I couldn't ask you too —"

"Nonsense!" cried Neil. He grabbed the lead from him. "You go ahead and we'll be right here."

Alun looked over at the shop door. In that moment, it was like staring into the gates of hell. With a heavy gulp, he made the brave walk inside.

As he went on to watch his new purchase being lifted up by the shopkeeper, he began to doubt his recent decision to embrace the spirit of Christmas. The act of giving to others was a wonderful prospect, but not at *this* price.

Alun could see the pair of supportive faces grinning at him from the other side of the window and they offered a thumbs-up. The accountant raised up his own thumb and muttered to the shopkeeper: "Can I make sure to get a receipt for that one, please?"

CHAPTER 12

Rhiannon pulled up outside the humble shop and turned off her car. It was even smaller than she had expected. How such a local shop could ever stay in business was beyond her understanding. She was no businessperson, but she was fairly certain that a shop required customers to make a profit, and there can't have been many of those in Llanlyn.

Fortunately for her, George had been able to walk home after their little visit to Enfys Bowen's house, and now it was time to start their new carpool routine (one where the driver had received a rather raw end of the deal).

The reporter climbed out of her vehicle and took a good look around at the grey stone that made up the row of houses on each side of the road. She saw the sign of a pub poking out in the far distance. Beer: another essential commodity, she thought.

As she entered the shop, a frantic George came stumbling down the stairs behind the counter. His hair was still in need of a comb, and he flung his coat across a very creased shirt.

"I'm so sorry!" he cried. "I didn't even hear your car."

"Calm down," said Rhiannon. "I'm just a little early." She inspected the limited selection of goods on offer and baulked at the prices. "Wow, people must really need their *Nutella* to pay that price."

"People seem to be willing to pay it," said George, grabbing himself a breakfast bar.

Rhiannon peered into the small fridge which contained an unappealing combination of milk and *Vimto*. "Mmmh," she muttered. "There's a term for that."

The intern munched away and thought about his answer: "Capitalism?"

His colleague shook her head. "More like daylight robbery."

They both headed for the car and decided to say nothing further on the subject. It wasn't long before the two commuters were crawling through the village, as Rhiannon took her time to take in all the sights. The only places of note seemed to be one public house, a primary school and a town hall.

The car continued its way out along a narrow country road, and the person in the passenger seat grew suspicious.

"Why are we going this way?" asked George, when it was clear they were taking a detour.

"I want to pay someone a little visit," Rhiannon replied.

The steep climb to Llechwedd Farm was enough to give Rhiannon a light flutter in her stomach. She was normally quite comfortable with heights but not when operating a moving vehicle, especially one that sounded like it was wailing out in protest.

When they reached the very top and pulled into the quiet yard, it was hard not to be impressed by the view. The village of Llanlyn now resembled a small model from the station's miniature railway, and, if they looked hard enough, they could just about make out the faint train line running towards the lake.

George lifted up the enormous lens attached to his camera and peered through the viewfinder.

"Can you see it?" Rhiannon asked.

"Yep," said George. With the help of his giant magnifier, he could quite clearly see the very same crossing that they had visited less than twenty-four hours earlier. The image was so crisp that the surrounding trees looked like they were rising up in a pop-up book.

Little did they know it, but these two trespassers were being spied upon themselves. Aranwen Hendry peered at the two people standing in her farmyard. When it came to her surroundings, she didn't miss a beat. Visitors were not common at Llechwedd Farm, and, unless they were delivering parcels, any stranger was treated with great suspicion.

The elderly woman made her way downstairs, as she heard the knock and swung the front door wide open to let in an ice-cold breeze.

"Mrs Hendry?" Rhiannon asked. "Sorry to bother you." She received an emotionless stare. "We're from the —"

"I know who you both are," said Mrs Hendry.

The journalist and her intern both turned to each other in surprise. "Oh, I see."

"I saw you yesterday." Her words made the visitors rather uncomfortable. "I spoke to Mrs Bowen shortly after you left her house. She filled me in on the details."

"Well," said Rhiannon. "I suppose that saves us some time." She could feel the warmth emanating out from the house and had hoped that she didn't need to ask her next question: "Do you mind if we come in?"

Mrs Hendry was thrown by the request. This situation was highly unusual, and she had completely forgotten her manners.

"Why, yes, of course." She escorted them both through into her front living room.

There was a smell in the air that reminded Rhiannon of her grandmother's house, and she believed it was the comforting aroma of freshly-cooked Lobscouse. What struck her the most about the room was the strange variety of ornaments on display: everything from a metallic crocodile sculpture to a miniature totem pole.

"You seem very well travelled," said Rhiannon, as she admired the pair of wooden clogs sitting on the mantelpiece.

Mrs Hendry seemed to enjoy the compliment. "Uh, yes. Although we haven't been to another country since our honeymoon to Shrewsbury. Everything you see here is from the charity shop."

Rhiannon had been so distracted by the sheer amount of artefacts (or "clutter" as her accountant friend would probably call it) that she had failed to notice that there was someone sleeping in one of the chairs.

"Oh!" she cried, having almost sat on the man. "Did you want us to use a different room?"

"Don't mind him," said Mrs Hendry. "My husband won't even notice that we've been in here. He sleeps like a log."

"Fair enough," said her awkward guest.

George was busy looking out of the window, his camera at the ready. "It's a great view you have up here," he said.

Mrs Hendry shrugged. "It's the only one I've ever known. This farm has been in my family for generations."

"I bet the view's changed a bit since the days of horse and carts," said Rhiannon with an amused smile.

The older woman didn't seem as amused. "Not really."

The journalist moved away from the sleeping man and crouched down on an old milking stool on the other side of the room. It was hard not to be distracted by Mr Hendry's peculiar snoring.

"Anyway," she said, "I imagine you probably know why we're here."

"Not really."

For a moment, Rhiannon had begun to wonder whether she was speaking to a robot whose vocal settings had become stuck.

"Oh, okay, then. Well, perhaps you might not be aware of the body that was found down at the railway line?"

"I know."

"Great! Let's start there. What exactly do you know, Mrs Hendry?"

"I know there was a body." Just as the reporter was about to stab herself in the face with a nearby poker tool, the woman spoke again. "I saw it before Enfys Bowen did."

Rhiannon sat up. "Wait — you saw it — when?"

"When I got up that morning," replied Mrs Hendry. "Every morning, I put on the kettle and have a look to see what everyone's up to."

"*Everyone*?"

"Yes. Enfys Bowen, Farmer Jones, Dil-Dolfach —"

"Okay, okay — so you did the rounds — then what? You saw the body?"

"Not straight away."

"Wait, what time was this?" Rhiannon took a deep breath. I need to calm down, she thought. *Keep it together, Rhiannon.*

"The sun was just coming up," said Mrs Hendry. "I'm an early bird, see."

"Right, so this was the crack of dawn. How long before you noticed the body?"

The woman pondered for a moment. "Right after I saw the man in yellow."

There was a short silence. Even George had turned his attention away from the window and was now hanging on the woman's every word.

"Man in yellow?" Rhiannon asked. Mrs Hendry nodded.
"How do you know it was a man?"

"Well, I don't, really. But he walked like a man. The person
was wearing a big, yellow raincoat."

"Did you see the face?"

Mrs Hendry shook her head. "His hood was fully up."

"Where was this person heading?"

"Back towards the station. I saw him walking along the
railway line. Nobody I recognised. Oh, and he was holding a
shovel."

"A shovel?" Had Rhiannon been offered a cup of tea, she
would have spat it out.

"Oh, yes. Very unusual. That's when I moved my binoculars
across and saw the red man."

"You mean, a person dressed as Father Christmas?"

Mrs Hendry paused. "Yes... now that you mention it, he did
look a bit like Father Christmas. But I stopped believing in him a
long time ago." The woman giggled to herself. It was the first
sign of emotion she had expressed so far.

"*Then* what happened?" asked Rhiannon.

"Then I finished making the tea."

The journalist hunched over on her stool and clutched her
own face.

"The next time I checked the window," Mrs Hendry continued, "I saw Enfys Bowen walking her dog. She stopped when
she reached the body. She didn't half look surprised."

"Did you also call the police?"

"Oh, no. It's none of my business. It's important to respect
people's privacy."

The journalist's eyes did a full roll inside their sockets.

In a burst of panic, Mr Hendry sprung up in his chair like a
fired catapult. The man's cry startled the guests, before he tried
to remember where he was. He didn't seem too fazed by the

strangers in his living room and was more concerned with the nightmare he had just experienced.

When Rhiannon emerged back outside again, she was quite relieved. Nothing could have prepared her for the strangeness of Mr and Mrs Hendry, but the visit might still have been worth it.

"Some people are absolutely bonkers," she said, once they were at a safe distance from the front door. The journalist turned to her intern to find him lying on the ground whilst trying to get a photo. "I rest my case."

George abandoned his attempt at an artistic shot and climbed to his feet. "Who do you think she saw in the yellow raincoat?"

Rhiannon looked out across at the enormous landscape stretching out below them. "Who knows... but that woman doesn't seem to miss anything around here. For all we know, she might have seen the killer walking away from the scene of the crime."

"If they had a shovel," said George, "why didn't they just bury the body?"

"That's a very twisted way of thinking, George." Rhiannon turned to him. "Any chance you own a yellow coat?"

The young man went pale, as he realised what she might be suggesting.

"Relax!" his colleague cried. "I'm only messing with you." She looked back at the house and shuddered. "She's probably watching us right now. Come on, let's get out of here. The sooner we're out of range, the better."

They headed towards the car and missed the appearance of someone in the window. Mrs Hendry lifted up her binoculars and followed their journey down the hill. It was shaping up to be quite a busy day, she thought.

CHAPTER 13

"Now, you *do* realise that I'm a wedding planner, don't you, Uncle Alun?"

The accountant sat opposite his relative's desk with a growing sense of trepidation. He was fully aware of what his cousin once removed did for a living, but he knew that her professional expertise was far more relevant than his own.

He had never arranged a party in his life and had been willing to make the special trip to Dolgellau out of pure desperation.

"Yes, I'm aware of that," he said, looking over at the enormous bridal dress hanging on a nearby mannequin. "But I was just hoping you could... point me in the right direction."

Lisa Hughes nodded with apparent understanding. She was like a wise medical professional, and her patient was in a very bad way indeed.

"Don't you worry, Uncle Al. We're going to get you through this. I'm here for you."

She grabbed his forearm and squeezed it with affection.

Alun breathed a sigh of relief. "Thank you."

"If I can't help a desperate family member at Christmas, then who can I help, eh?" She looked at him with that same expression that his cousin always possessed. It was a look of sheer pity, as if the lives of everyone else in the world were a despicable mess. "Right, then!" She clapped her hands and stood up in a burst of enthusiasm. Her sudden change in tone made her relative jump. "What are we dealing with? Formal affair? Casual? House party?"

Alun racked his brains for an answer. "Uh, does it have to be either of those things?"

Lisa rushed over to him and placed a concerned hand on his shoulder. "Oh, Uncle Alun. You poor thing." She marched into the centre of the room and held her hands up towards the ceiling like an artist trying to express their vision. "This isn't just a Christmas party we're talking about."

"It's not?" Alun asked.

"No! This is an opportunity to offer people an evening they will never forget — an experience of a lifetime!" She grabbed a piece of fabric and turned it into an elegant shawl around her neck. "Are you familiar with Fitzgerald?"

"The bar and grill?"

"The writer..."

"Oh. Yes, well... I think so."

Alun braced himself, as the woman in her early twenties came running at him before stopping just short of knocking the man off his chair. She grabbed his head as though it were a crystal ball. "You, Alun, are like Gatsby!"

"I am?"

Lisa nodded and tilted his head up. "Say it..."

"Excuse me?"

"Say it!" she cried. "Say that you're Gatsby!"

"I'm Gatsby..."

"Louder!"

"I am the Great Gatsby!" Alun cried out.

"Yes! That's more like it!" His cousin did a little dance before placing her hands together. "I think we're ready." She grabbed her notepad and began scribbling. "You're going to need mood... some entertainment! What sort of venue are we working with?"

"I was just thinking we could have the party in the office," said Alun with a shrug.

Lisa burst out laughing. "That's funny, Uncle Al. Very funny. But, seriously, what sort of space?" She saw his blank stare. "Oh... you *are* being serious. Okay, well, at least we have control. Is there a photocopier?"

"Uh, yes. Why do you ask?"

"Every office Christmas party needs a photocopier. Just trust me. Right, I'm thinking we stick with the office theme and heighten everything a little. Make it ironic. It can still have that chic-ness."

The accountant's head was spinning. "*Chic*?"

"Have you thought about the music playlist yet?" Lisa asked.

"Not really, why?"

The young woman held up her hand as if she were about to season a dish of food. "I need to know the atmos before I can plan the look. Are we thinking hip-hop or something more chill?"

Alun had a think. "Shaking Stevens?"

"Mmh," said Lisa, jotting the name down. "I'll have to check him out. He sounds more drum and bass."

"I don't want to ruin the flow," said her cousin. "But how much does something like this usually cost?"

"Well, that depends..." Lisa grabbed a chair and sat on it backwards to face him. "What's your budget?"

The question had floored the accountant. He, of all people, should have thought about a budget and was rather embarrassed to be so unprepared.

"Well —"

"Ah, ah, ahhh!" Lisa placed her pen against his lips to silence him and lifted up her notepad. "You don't have to say it out loud if you don't want to. Sometimes that can jinx everything. Just write me down a ballpark figure, and we'll see what we can do.

Alun nodded and jotted down a number that was barely three figures. It was a sight that made the wedding planner want to yell out in horror.

"We can add a little extra for the sausage rolls and stuff," he said. "I wouldn't want to skimp on those."

Only moments later, Alun was standing outside the building again. Lisa had almost seemed insulted, and it turned out that blood wasn't always thicker than water when it came to business.

The accountant took one last look at his relative's wedding shop and sighed. He hopped into his blue Beetle with a great, big tail hanging between his legs.

As he saw the town of Dolgellau rising up in his rear view mirror, the accountant had a sudden thought. Perhaps the trip didn't have to be a wasted one, after all. With a slight detour to his journey home, he found himself approaching the tiny village of Llanlyn.

"How lovely to see you back here," said Lowri Medwyn, as she greeted the accountant entering her gift shop. "To what do we owe the pleasure this time?"

Alun approached the shelf full of train models and rubbed his chin. "I just thought I'd pick up something," he said. "Seeing as I'm passing through."

"Caught the bug, have we?" Lowri gave him a sly grin.

It took a moment before the man realised what she was implying. "Oh, no! It's nothing like that. I'm just –"

"You're not the first, and you won't be the last. It's nothing to be ashamed of."

Her embarrassed customer ignored the judgemental stare and turned his attention back to the models.

"Gosh," said Lowri. "It's been a quiet one, this Christmas. We're normally run off our feet this time of year."

"Do you think it could have something to do with, you know... the incident on the line?"

"Well, who knows? It can't have helped, I'm sure." She lifted up a copy of *The Merioneth Press* newspaper. "Parents don't like reading about dead Santas. I don't know why they print such rubbish!"

Alun was suddenly very glad that his journalist friend wasn't also in attendance on this occasion. Otherwise, things might have become ugly.

"They only print what they think will sell," he said.

"I can't understand it," said Lowri, shaking her head at the headline again. "It's certainly not doing our operation any good."

"Oooh! You have farm animals, too!" Alun rushed over to a display of figurines and realised he had forgotten himself. "For the kids, obviously."

Lowri raised her eyebrow. "Whatever you say, Mr Hughes."

The accountant re-emerged from the shop with a carrier bag in each hand. The quick stop-off at Llanlyn Station had been a successful visit, he thought, and he turned his focus to the old station room. Perhaps a little inspiration was also in order. He began to wonder whether his subconscious had planned this visit all along, like the brain of an addict trying to feed that obsessive craving, bubbling under the surface.

Just as he was about to cross the platform, he was faced with a furious looking station master. Dyfed Simon was pacing up and down, tutting and grunting to himself, whilst checking his watch. "Damn and blast!" he cried.

"Is everything alright?" asked Alun on his way past.

"No — it's not alright!" Dyfed roared. The station master saw the terrified expression on the other man's face and realised who he was talking to. The last thing he wanted to do was lose any more customers, and he tried to calm himself down. "I'm sorry, it's just... we're running late again!"

Alun turned to the railway line and noticed the absence of any trains. It was hard to imagine any passengers being too upset over a delayed steam train, he thought. They weren't exactly using the service to commute to work, but something told him that it was best to remain quiet. The station master was already red in the face, and any gesture of consolation had the risk of causing offence.

"And do you know whose fault this all is?" Dyfed asked. The other man shook his head. "That useless conductor!"

Alun could picture the man he was referring to. The conductor he had met previously was not exactly a stickler for timekeeping. In fact, it was a miracle they had set-off at all by the time he had checked their tickets for the umpteenth time.

The accountant decided it was best not to keep the man any longer than was necessary, and he probably just needed some time to cool off. After leaving the irate station master to spit his feathers in peace, he headed straight for the sanctuary of the engine room.

The model railway was exactly how he had left it: a world so much more peaceful than his own. If Alun had any hope of replicating the structure's calming nature, he needed to first spend as much time in its presence as possible. If all was to go to plan, he too might hope to become the master of his own kingdom.

As the man moved closer to inspect the various pieces that allowed this tiny railway to operate, he was struck by an unexpected figure in the corner.

"Oh!" the man in overalls cried. "I didn't see you!"

Twm, a giant of a man, had been frozen in place for the last

ten minutes. There was something about the miniature railway
that hypnotised this thirty-year-old until he was barely aware of
his surroundings.

"Likewise," said Alun. "I didn't mean to disturb you."

The tall apprentice had a sudden look of panic on his face
and grabbed the broom lying down on the ground. "I'm
supposed to be sweeping!" he cried and began frantically
attacking the floor with his brush.

Alun stared at this nervous individual and realised that there
was an innocence he had not detected before. After listening to
him speak a few more times, it was as though he was engaging
with a wide-eyed child in a powerful man's body. There was no
denying Twm was an imposing figure, with his giant frame and
tree trunk legs, but his demeanour was more like that of a
four-year-old.

"I have to sweep here first — then the platform — then the
café!"

"That's a lot of sweeping," said Alun.

Twm nodded. "Everything has to be swept."

"Do you not get to ride the train?"

Alun's question had caught the other man off guard, and a
confused Twm looked over at the passing model train.

"Not *that* train," Alun added, quickly. "I mean, the big
train."

His last sentence caused a whirlwind of emotion in the
apprentice's head. "No," he muttered. "I never get to ride the
train! Ever!"

The engine room went silent for a moment, as his words
continued to echo for quite some time.

"Oh," said the accountant. "I'm sorry to hear that."

"He never lets me ride the train!" Twm cried. "He never lets
me do *anything*!"

Alun saw the broom handle start to buckle under the

immense pressure. "You like model railways?" he asked, trying to change the mood.

Twm's broad shoulders began to loosen, as he gazed fondly over the impressive display. "This is my favourite place," he said.

"I can see why," said Alun. "It's the best place I've ever seen!"

Twm smiled and appeared to let his guard down. Both men, as different as they might have seemed, were exactly on the same page. The model railway was the greatest place in the world (at least, as far as they were concerned).

"Have you seen the boat?" Twm asked with a burst of excitement.

The accountant was excited too, and he waited for the big man to climb over the small fence. In a matter of seconds, he was on all fours amongst the plastic cows and began fiddling away with the small canal boat floating in a narrow river. After an initial struggle, the tiny motor erupted into life, and the barge went chugging across the water on its own.

A tiny tear began forming in Alun's eye, as he watched the boat cruise along at a steady pace. "Oh, that's good! That's very, very good..."

The two giddy men began chuckling away, blissfully unaware of the shadow in the open doorway.

"Twm!!" a voice roared at the top of his lungs.

The startled apprentice jumped and fell backwards against a miniature farm house, crushing it in the process with his large backside.

"Twm!!" the voice cried again, and a furious Iestyn came running across the room with his arms flailing. "What have you done?"

The engineer reached across the fence to grab the fallen man by the arms.

"You stupid man! You've broken it!"

"Argh! I'm sorry, sorry, sorry! Sorry, sorry, sorry!"

Twm's whimpering reminded Alun of a scared puppy. He observed the chaotic interaction with a mixture of shock and guilt. Had he not been so curious, the entire accident may never have happened.

"Get up! Get up, you big lump!" Iestyn kept struggling to haul the man up. Twm was almost paralysed with fear over the destruction caused by his sore backside and did nothing to help the person trying to pull him away.

Once the apprentice was safely out of harm's way, the engineer had to take a seat and catch his breath. "I told you never to come in here!" he hissed. "Look what happens when you don't do as you're told!"

"It's not his fault." The two volunteers in blue overalls turned to look at the accountant, who was slowly approaching them with the timidness of a small bird. "I asked to see the boat move. You can blame me."

Iestyn glared at him with a grunt. "I remember you," he said. "You're nothing but trouble."

Alun was taken aback. The only "trouble" he had ever been accused of was when he'd accidentally left a gate open. "That's certainly not my intention. I'm just intrigued by model railways."

There was another grunt. "I suggest you stay clear of models from now on. You've done enough damage to this one."

The accountant nodded. He could see there was not much use in defending himself. "Well," he said. "I'd better let you both go."

"Yes, I think you'd better have."

Alun turned his back on them and began heading towards the exit. Just as he approached the doorway, the accountant paused and looked down at his shopping bags. "Oh," he said. "There was this one thing I wanted to ask you about..."

The furious engineer, who was still seated on the floor with an exhausted face, stared at him. This annoying man had a lot of nerve, he thought, and he had better choose his question very wisely.

Alun coughed and pulled out one of the model trains. He skimmed the back of the box briefly and raised it into the air. "Do you know anything about electric accessory decoders?"

CHAPTER 14

Rhiannon lifted up the newspaper and read the headline: *Dead Santa*. It was hardly subtle, but she expected nothing less from her editor-in-chief.

"Couldn't have asked for a better Christmas present, hey Rhiannon?"

Morgan Morris was standing above his reporter's desk with a beaming smile. His eyes were filled with a pair of pound signs, and he waited for her reaction.

"Wow," she said. "You've really outdone yourself this time, Chief."

"I know!" Morgan cried. "Haven't I? With a headline like that, you barely need the article!"

"Exactly!" the journalist cried back. "Why do I even bother?"

The editor rubbed his hands together before raising them high into the air. "Now! I've been thinking..."

Oh, dear, Rhiannon thought. That was never a good sign. She always braced herself when her boss had been "thinking".

"We do a follow-up," Morgan continued. "But *this* time, we give the public what they want."

"A blank page?"

"A proper photograph!"

Rhiannon checked the front page again. "But we *have* a photograph. George and I were at the scene of the crime."

Her editor lifted up the newspaper. "This is just an empty railway track! Nothing interesting about that."

Good job George wasn't nearby, she thought to herself. He had spent hours rooting through all those location shots.

"So what do you suggest?" she asked. "A sheep? A tractor? Or how about this — a sheep *driving* a tractor? That would be a lot more interesting."

Morgan paused for a moment. "Correct me if I'm wrong, but I think you might be pulling my leg, aren't you?" His reporter didn't even bother to respond, so the man continued: "Now imagine this — we give the reader an actual photo of the body!"

Rhiannon was very confused. "*Whose* body? Hefin Charles'?"

"Forget about Hefin Charles," said Morgan. "The general public don't care about *him*! What they really care about is the character he was portraying."

"Santa? You want to print a photograph of a dead Santa on the front page?!"

Morgan clapped his hands together. "*Now* you're seeing it! Boom! What do you think?"

"I think printing a photo of a bloodied Santa Clause is probably not the best idea."

The editor gave her an innocent shrug. "It's both shocking — *and* festive. What more could you want?"

Rhiannon shook her head in disgust. "Where would we even get a photo like that?"

"All you need is a good costume and a bottle of ketchup!" Morgan patted her on the shoulder. "I'm sure you and George can figure something out."

The editor left his employee stewing behind her desk. This newspaper never ceased to amaze her. Lying some poor volunteer down in the dirt whilst they were dressed in a Santa costume was not how she had envisaged spending her Christmas.

"Do you have a moment?"

Rhiannon looked up to see George standing there with a plastic card in his hand.

"It depends," she said. "Does it involve photographing dead Santas?"

The confused intern stared at her. "Excuse me?"

She didn't bother to explain and joined her intern over at his desk. The sight of his meticulously arranged IT equipment and spotless workspace made her want to gag. What was so wrong with a bit of clutter?

"So I've gone through yesterday's photos," said George, opening up a folder on his desktop.

"That must have taken a while," said Rhiannon. "You only took a *million* pictures."

The photographer ignored what was a grossly inaccurate estimation in his opinion (it was more around the thousand mark) and began flicking through a series of images.

They watched all the familiar locations whizz by, many of them captured during the long walk down the railway line, until the carousel imagery stopped.

"There! That's one." George pointed towards what appeared to be an empty train track, disappearing off into the distance.

Rhiannon leant forward and squinted at the photograph. "Am I missing something? I spent enough time staring at that thing. I'm pretty familiar with it."

"Look closer," said George.

Any closer and her forehead would have been squashed up against the screen, Rhiannon thought. "If it's some Chaffinch you're trying to show me, then you can forget it."

The intern sighed and zoomed in with the help of his mouse.

With a section of the image now fully enlarged, the journalist almost gasped. Lurking in the background of the photograph was a figure in a hooded, yellow raincoat.

"You're kidding," the journalist muttered. "Wait, when was this one taken?"

"It's from the crossing. We're looking in the direction of the station."

Rhiannon's heart was starting to beat quicker than it had done since her drive up to Llechwedd Farm. The stranger's face was shrouded in darkness, but it was clearly looking at her.

"So this person was probably following us?" she asked.

George nodded. "What do you reckon this means?"

His colleague let the discovery marinate a little in her mind and grabbed her coat. "I reckon it's time we got some lunch."

The breeze of fresh air was exactly what the two had needed. They headed straight for the centre of town, which was quite busy for a weekday, and the festive lights were all in full glow above the heads of eager shoppers looking for a head start.

"Who do you think he is?" asked George, when they emerged from the local bakery with hot pasties in their hands.

"*He*?" asked Rhiannon before taking a bite of her scolding-hot filling.

"Mrs Hendry said she thought it was a man."

"Mrs Hendry is off her trolley."

George paused. He couldn't argue with *that*. Anyone who spent their days spying on people from such a great distance may not have possessed the soundest of minds.

"For all we know," Rhiannon continued, "it could be the killer underneath that hood."

"Why would they return to the scene of the crime?" asked George.

His colleague shrugged. "Leaving a dead body dressed from head to toe in bright red next to a railway line wasn't the most clever move. We're not exactly dealing with the smartest person in the world. There's no reason for them to change now."

They walked towards the town square and saw a Father Christmas sitting in a pop-up grotto.

"I've seen that guy before," said Rhiannon.

George was hesitant about telling her that the figure she was looking at was in fact Santa Clause, a person many people would have seen before. But he knew better than to challenge his superior's intelligence.

"Father Christmas?" he asked.

Rhiannon glared at him. "I'm talking about the bloke *underneath* the costume."

"Oh, right."

"Unless..." The journalist pretended to look horrified. "Goodness! Has nobody ever told you the truth about Santa Clause yet, George? Wait, how old did you say you were again?"

The intern blushed. "Yes, I'm aware."

"Phew!" She began walking in the direction of the grotto. "Now, come on. Time to tell him what we want for Christmas."

Hari Malwen had been having a dreadful afternoon. Not only did he possess the worst hangover known to man, but he still had another two hours to go before he could deflate his grotto and call it a day. The children he had spoken to so far had all been a nuisance, and his donations bucket was looking emptier than his rumbling stomach. Pengower town square was normally prime real estate when it came to making a little extra over the Christmas period, but that day, the general public were even more tight-fisted than usual.

As he prepared to greet his next stingy punter, he was surprised to find that the person standing in front of him was a lot older than he was used to.

"Hello, Big Man." Rhiannon towered over the bearded individual with folded arms and a stern face. "I've been wanting to talk to you."

The Santa Clause grumbled and felt the palms of his hands begin to moisten. "Not again... you people have no respect for a person's workplace. I'm trying to do an honest day's living over here! This is harassment."

"Calm down, St Nicholas. I'm not with the police."

Hari let out a deep breath. "Thank God for that. Well, you can clear off, then."

"How dare you," said Rhiannon. "I'm just a mother trying to speak with Father Christmas."

The man gave her a suspicious frown. "I can't see any children. No children — no Santa!"

"George!" The journalist signalled for the young man hiding behind her to come forward. "I'm afraid he's a bit shy."

Hari sniggered. "You have to be joking!"

The intern hunched over and tried to step away. "I really don't think —"

"Come along," said his colleague. "Sit down on the man's knee."

"Get away!" Hari cried, as the other man was being pushed towards him. "Both of you — get out!"

The grotto went silent, and Rhiannon allowed her intern to move away.

"What if I make you a very generous donation?" she asked, hovering a ten-pound note above his collection bucket.

The gesture seemed to get Hari's attention. "I don't even know what you want!"

"Tell me about Llanlyn Station," Rhiannon said. "You seem like a bloke who keeps his ear to the ground. Have you ever noticed anything strange?"

"I've no idea!" Hari snapped. "I barely know the place."

"You were a last-minute replacement for their missing Santa."

The man had to readjust his artificial beard in order to hide his surprise. "Exactly. It was last-minute. Clearly, I wasn't their first choice, which tells you how involved I was with the place."

"Nice little earner, though." Rhiannon smiled. "It must be very competitive in your line of work."

"At least it's honest — unlike your seedy job."

"I'd hardly call impersonating a man who climbs down chimneys honest, would you?"

Rhiannon was leaning forward into his personal space, when she sensed a presence behind her.

"Hurry up!" cried the impatient mother at the beginning of a growing line. "You've had your turn!"

The journalist popped another note into the bucket and gave the woman behind her a threatening stare.

"Anyway," she said, having returned to her audience with Santa Clause. "Did you know the man you replaced?"

Hari shook his head and the beard slipped down. "He wasn't on the circuit as far as I knew. We professionals usually stick together. I'm pretty sure he was an amateur."

Rhiannon glanced down at the half-empty bottle of coke beside his leg. "Well, glad to know I'm talking to a pro..."

Hari let out a chesty smoker's cough. "I've been doing this job long enough to know when people won't last. It's harder than it looks."

"It's a bit hard to keep it up when you're dead." Her remark made the man go silent for a moment, and she knew it would. "So, what does a Santa like you do for the rest of the year?"

"This and that," said Hari.

"*This and that*?"

"I've got my fingers in a lot of pies." The man chuckled. "Or mince pies, even!"

Rhiannon let out an exaggerated laugh. "Yes, very good! Ho, ho, ho... What kind of pies are we talking about?"

Hari sighed. This woman clearly wasn't going to give up. "I'm in antiques."

"Antiques?"

"Yeah, you know — old stuff."

The journalist folded up her arms. "Don't get all technical on me now. You sound like such a specialist."

"I've always had a good eye when it comes to valuable goods. You'll often see me down the market here on a Saturday."

"I don't recognise you," Rhiannon said. "But maybe it's just the big beard and hat."

"I've got quite the reputation for shifting stuff."

"I bet you have."

"If people have something they want selling or valued, they come to old Hari."

"I shall have to take your number."

George turned to his colleague in surprise.

The Santa imposter cackled and coughed before reaching inside his pocket. He began jotting down a number in his notebook and ripped off the page.

"You make sure to get in touch if you need me."

The journalist took the number like a person being handed a muddy spoon.

"How thoughtful of you," she said.

Hari grinned to reveal a mouth full of rotten teeth. "What can I say — it's Christmas!"

His two visitors left the grotto with disgusted faces.

"Well, that bloke's definitely on the naughty list," Rhiannon said, as they walked across the town square.

"Do you think he's connected to Hefin's murder?" asked George.

"A Santa knocking off another Santa? I've seen stranger things."

"Maybe that person in the yellow coat was just a trainspotter."

"Well, they *are* famous for wearing raincoats."

They turned down a side street leading back to the office, when Rhiannon felt her phone vibrating. She pulled it out and checked the caller: Sally.

The new sergeant at Pengower police station, Sally Harris, and *The Merioneth Press*' lead reporter had formed a rather unlikely friendship over the last few weeks. Having first met each other at a certain (and rather unforgettable) fancy dress party at Penny Hall, the two had bonded over a mutual struggle to find their place amongst this small community and its variety of local inhabitants.

Both women had only recently relocated from life in a big city, where a person could quite easily remain anonymous for as long as they wished.

Rhiannon and Sally's casual, new relationship also came with significant benefits towards their chosen professions: one of them could provide a string of useful leads, whilst the other had a far superior knowledge of local gossip and residents.

The journalist answered her call with a natural feeling of curiosity. A police sergeant was unlikely to ring for a quick chat about the weather, and she hoped that her extensive assistance in a recent murder investigation was about to pay her back.

"I just need to take this," she said and crouched down beside a lamppost.

George waited very patiently for his colleague to finish, as she hummed and nodded to the continuous voice in her ear.

"Thanks for the update, Sally. Are we still on for curry-night next Wednesday?"

Rhiannon terminated her call and stood up to greet her

intern. She had a burning fire in her eyes, the kind a person got when they were sitting on some exciting new information.

"Everything alright?" asked George.

"They've confirmed Hefin's cause of death," said Rhiannon.

"But we already know that, though, don't we?"

The journalist shook her head. "He didn't die from a blow to the head." She paused, partly for effect and partly because she was still processing the news herself. "Hefin Charles died from a gunshot wound."

CHAPTER 15

The package sitting outside Alun's front door filled him with a buzz that would rival any thrill-seeking activity or recreational drug. Who needed a death-defying jump when you had a highly-anticipated delivery on your doorstep? Normally, his courier's insistence on leaving parcels unattended outside his house would have filled him with utter frustration, but on this occasion, the delivery person was forgiven. For Alun knew that the contents of this unmarked package contained the key elements of his new project.

Peg greeted him as she always did (with an excited bark and a wagging tail) and followed him upstairs into the spare room. Sitting in the corner was a box he had retrieved the night before from the confines of his attic. A cloud of dust sprang into the air, as he ripped it open and sniffed in that damp and musty smell. Inside was an object that he had not seen in many years, and it had aged far better than he had. The model steam train his grandfather had bought him could finally make its maiden journey, he thought, after years of neglect and a lack of additional parts.

A train needed a railway, and although an eight-year-old

Alun Hughes may not have been fortunate enough to build upon this first step into a smaller world, the adult Alun Hughes was about to more than make up for it. He was well aware that many people, including his journalist-friend, would have a term to describe his new obsession. But the accountant was adamant that the only crisis he had experienced that week was choosing between a miniature barn or a stable.

The spare room had been intended for visitors only, but seeing as he had never had any guests over in the first place, it was time to make good use of this wasted space. The Border Collie witnessed her master laying his train track with a nose rested against her paws (almost as though she was concerned about the man's mental well-being).

Alun continued to build for many hours, until a loud ringtone on the other side of the room broke off his concentration. He paused for a moment to admire his rather basic feat of engineering before reaching across the room to grab his phone.

"Hello?" he asked, having maintained the tradition of not just checking the name of the caller on his small screen.

"What are you doing right this second?" asked the familiar voice.

Alun looked over at the train track snaking across the carpet. "Uh, nothing much. Why?"

"How do you fancy a little car ride?" Rhiannon's voice asked.

An hour later, Alun was sitting in the back seat of his friend's vehicle and bound for the little village of Llanlyn. The front seat was already taken by the young photojournalist, who was making use of his lift home and listening to the strange song coming from his driver's car radio.

"Now here's a riddle for you," said Rhiannon, tapping her fingers to the sound of "The Riddle" by Nik Kershaw. "You know this one?" George shook his head. "Fair enough. It's a little before my time too, but you can't beat a classic like this. So what kind of music do you like?"

The intern had to think about it for a moment. "I quite like Ed Sheeran."

Before his disappointed driver could come up with an appropriate response, Alun leaned forward, popping his head in between them. "Can we go back to the gunshot?" he asked. "You're sure she definitely said gunshot?"

"No," said Rhiannon. "The cause of death was bad cholesterol." She ignored the confused look from her intern. "Course it was a gunshot."

The accountant rolled his eyes. "What kind of bullet was it?"

"The kind that passes through you at great speed."

"What I mean is — are we talking about a shotgun pellet or an actual bullet?"

"How on earth should I know? I'm not an armourer. All that matters is that Hefin Charles was shot point blank."

Alun sat back into his chair and stared out of the window at the passing scenery. "This changes everything."

"It doesn't really," said his driver. "A man is still dead. And the killer hasn't changed identities all of a sudden. All that's different is the murder weapon."

"What it now means is that the murderer had an opportunity to kill him from a distance. Hefin might not have even been aware of who killed him."

"I'm sure he wasn't," said Rhiannon. "Nobody is aware of anything when you're dead."

The accountant couldn't argue with that one. Even with her back facing him, he could still sense his friend's smug smile. She seemed to love getting the last word in.

"What about the blow to the head?" asked George.

"That might have been caused by the fall," said Alun. "He

could have easily hit his head against something hard once he'd been shot."

"Like a train track?" asked their driver.

"Maybe," Alun replied, trying not to sound annoyed. "But his head wasn't lying against the railway line as far as we know." He paused to give it some more thought. There was nothing like a car journey to get his mind whirling. "Unless he was moved afterwards..."

Rhiannon made a sound that harked back to an old television cliffhanger. "Ooooh... this really is like one of your conundrums, isn't it Georgie Boy?" She nudged her passenger in the arm. "No parachutes this time though, eh?"

"Well," said Alun, "*technically*, there wasn't a parachute involved in the riddle, either."

"That's very true," said George, innocently turning to his driver. "The man died because he was *without* a parachute."

And just like that, the smugness had shifted to the back of the car. Alun sat there with a big grin on his face. He knew it would swing back eventually.

Their driver let out a long groan. "You're both as bad as each other," she said. "Honestly, how did I get stuck in a car with you two?"

The two men looked at each other with sheepish faces.

There was silence for the remaining duration of their journey, and the intern felt quite relieved to see his home above the village corner shop.

"Last stop!" Rhiannon cried, before mimicking the sound of a train whistle. "All passengers to depart!" Alun made a grab for the door handle. "Not you, obviously." The accountant froze and slowly returned to his seat.

"Thanks, Rhiannon." George left the vehicle and headed towards the shop.

The light was already beginning to fade, and the car continued to sit there with the engine running.

"He's a good lad," said Rhiannon, once the two friends were alone. "Just don't tell him I said that. You've got to keep these youngsters on their toes."

"There's a shop in Llanlyn?" asked Alun.

"I know, right? Who knew? And there's a cosy, little pub round the corner."

The accountant liked the sound of that. He could murder a nice pub meal with a pint of local beer. "Is that the plan, then?"

"What, go to the pub?" Rhiannon let out a laugh. "Yeah, you wish! I thought we could pay the station another little visit."

Alun could not have been more disappointed, especially as he had already been there that day. He would have mentioned that fact, but he knew it would only lead to more questions, and he wasn't quite ready to tell her about the new railway line just yet. Instead, he sat there and waited for her to pull away.

"What are you waiting for?" she eventually asked.

"Mmh?" her passenger asked, who had remained seated.

Rhiannon looked at him through her rearview mirror. "I'm not driving you around like a chauffeur!"

"But I've already got my seatbelt on." He saw the stern glare coming from the reflection and sighed. "Oh, alright."

He climbed out of the vehicle and jumped into the front passenger seat.

The village was deathly quiet at this time of day, and they passed through without seeing a single person. Once they had entered the station car park, the sun was now an orange glow above the surrounding hills.

"Do you think anybody will be here?" Alun asked, as they left the warmth of their vehicle and braved the freezing temperature outside.

"They should have closed about half an hour ago," said

Rhiannon, leading the way over a closed gate. The accountant couldn't tell if it was the unnecessary climb that made him hesitate or the fact that a closed gate usually meant they weren't supposed to enter.

"What exactly are we supposed to be looking for?" he asked, almost slipping his foot on the icy timber.

"Anything suspicious."

Great, Alun thought to himself. The last thing he ever wanted to look for was something "suspicious". That usually came with trouble, and he was never looking for trouble.

The platform was as empty as it had been earlier on, only now the café and gift shop windows were dark and unwelcoming. All the volunteers had clearly gone home, as far as they could see, and Doris, the steam train, had been put to bed for a well-earned night's rest.

As the two trespassers wandered around the empty station, Alun began to wonder whether the model railway was still accessible. Another peek surely couldn't have hurt, and it would have made the whole trip worthwhile.

"Did you want to check the old engine room?" he asked.

Rhiannon stared at him with a frown. "Where that toy train set is hiding, you mean?"

"Ah," said Alun, trying not to let her description of the great masterpiece hurt him inside. "I'd forgotten about that."

The journalist hated having her intelligence insulted, and she pointed towards the old building further down the platform. "Off you go then," she said. "Eat your heart out."

Alun hesitated to make sure that she was being serious, and then proceeded to scurry off like a giddy school boy. His friend shook her head and began peering through the various murky windows.

The accountant reached his destination with crushing disappointment flooding his entire body. He gazed down at the giant padlock keeping him from his fix of pleasure. It was as though he had developed an escalating new addiction, and some cruel person had staged an intervention.

He shook the closed doors just to make sure and walked away in defeat. Around the next corner was an old, abandoned steam engine. It sat amongst the overgrowth looking sad and lonely, having lost all purpose with its rusted components and peeled paint. Alun almost wanted to comfort the neglected loco-motive with a gentle pat against the side of its deteriorated cab.

"You poor thing," he muttered under his breath. For a split second, he could have sworn he was being watched, and it wasn't by the old train with a sorry face. The man checked behind him to find nothing but an old carriage covered in weeds. He approached the shattered windows to see what was inside. As he poked his head through the small opening, his face was coated in a layer of spider-web which caused him to dart back in horror. The man coughed and spluttered, patting himself down to shake off every last remaining dead fly. He had warned his dog on many occasions about sticking her head through mysterious holes. Now he had broken the cardinal sin himself and was paying the price.

Alun decided it was a good time to head back towards the safety of the open platform and strolled around yet another mysterious building with that same red brickwork. As he took a quick shortcut through a narrow passageway, the accountant heard a pair of footsteps moving very quickly towards him. He barely had a chance to turn around before this mysterious person grabbed him from behind.

CHAPTER 16

Alun's cry echoed across the entire station. He fell backwards against the wall, as the person who startled him continued to hold on tight. The smell of a familiar perfume wafted up his nostrils.

"*Your* face!" Rhiannon cried, roaring with laughter, as she pinned him against the wall. "Why does that never get old?!"

Her friend was inclined to point out that the joke most certainly *had* become old but was just glad to still be alive. He took a moment to recover from the immense shock, whilst Rhiannon enjoyed her victory.

"Please don't do that again," said Alun, checking his heart rate with a trembling finger.

"I'm sorry," said the amused journalist. "I couldn't resist." She squinted at him for a moment and flicked his hair. "Are those cobwebs?"

The grumpy accountant refused to answer. "Find anything interesting?"

"Nothing," said Rhiannon, pulling out a pack of cigarettes. "Don't judge me. I'm quitting after Christmas. No point starting before the new year."

Alun wanted to point out that it wasn't a judgemental stare he was giving her but a look of contemplation at having a cigarette himself (he certainly needed *something* to calm his nerves). He settled for a deep inhalation of cold, winter air instead and thought about suggesting a quick stop-off at the pub.

They walked back underneath the Victorian-style canopy hanging above the platform, and it became apparent that every-thing had already gone dark. The winter night had truly set in, and just as the two wanderers prepared to leave, they noticed a warm light coming from the signal box. They both looked at each other and made the cautious walk to the bottom of the stairs.

"Someone's still here," said Alun.

"So it would seem," said Rhiannon, making her first step towards the light. "Are you coming?"

Her friend knew by this point in their relationship that such a question was not really a question at all (but more like a command). He begrudgingly followed her up the stairs, until they reached the signal box door.

Rhiannon hushed her lips and tried to get a look through the window. Inside, a man was sitting with his feet up whilst listening to music coming out of a pair of speakers. She gave Alun another *hush* signal and barged through the door with the force of a police squadron during a raid.

The man inside the signal box went flying off his chair in fright and landed on the floor with a heavy *thud*. "For the love of —" He turned around to see the two strangers in the doorway.

Rhiannon really *did* enjoy giving people a heart attack, Alun thought, and he felt a great deal of sympathy for him.

"What are you doing here?" asked the man.

"We could ask you the same question," said Rhiannon. She

couldn't help but notice all the rubbish scattered across the floor. The song "Perfect 10" by The Beautiful South continued to play in the background.

"I'm a signalman, and this is a signal box! It doesn't take a genius..."

Alun recognised his face from the group they had seen at the café. He also noticed a sleeping bag and a suitcase over in the corner.

"There are no trains running as far as I can see," said Rhiannon. "Unless you do a night service now."

"You must be Eben," said Alun.

The signalman looked surprised. "How do you know my name?" he asked.

"A little birdy," said Rhiannon.

Alun gave her a disapproving frown. She had always enjoyed these games a lot more than he did. "We're not here to cause trouble. We've been investigating the death of Hefin Charles."

"You're police?!" Eben cried, cowering on the floor.

"More like press," Rhiannon muttered. She looked over at her associate. "As well as... accountancy support." She received another frown. "Oh, sorry. I almost forgot — he also does financial planning."

Eben crawled back to his chair, where a microphone was propped up in front of an audio mixer full of colourful dials. "Well," he said, "you won't find any answers up here. Nobody tells me anything."

"Isn't that a bit unusual for a signal person?" Rhiannon asked. "Normally you people have to know everything."

"Only if it has an impact on the train line," said Eben. "We're not usually filled in about *murders*."

"So you think he was murdered?"

The signalman threw her a furious glare. Her accusational

tone had not gone unnoticed. "*Everybody* knows he was murdered!" He lifted up a scrunched-up copy of *The Merioneth Press*. "It's in the bloody paper!"

"Glad to see that you're a fan of my work," said Rhiannon, slightly impressed that someone actually bothered to read it.

"You're telling me *you* wrote this tripe?" asked Eben.

The journalist stepped forward, until she was towering above the man. "Every... single... word..."

Her attempt to intimidate him had worked, and the nervous man swung his chair around to avoid eye contact.

"No wonder you're crawling around stations in the middle of the night," Eben muttered.

"*You* can talk," snapped Rhiannon. "Don't you have a home to go to?"

There was a short pause.

"Actually, I don't." The signalman's mood changed, and he began to sulk. "If you must know, my wife kicked me out four months ago."

"You've been sleeping here for four months?" asked Alun in horror. He had stayed in his auntie's caravan once and that was as rough as he ever wanted to sleep. There was nothing that gave him more comfort than the tranquillity of his own bed. In fact, he was looking forward to being reacquainted with it at that very moment.

"What else am I supposed to do?" Eben asked. "I've lost everything: my job, my house, my wife..." He let the song in the background fade out before putting on another track. "I've been on the air for thirty years."

"Wait a minute..." Alun stepped forward to get a better look at the man. "I knew I recognised your voice. You're DJ Bull!"

Eben unleashed the first smile since his guests had arrived. "The one and only!"

"DJ — what?" asked Rhiannon.

"Bull," Alun replied.

"You can say that again."

A confused Alun ignored her and went back to fanboying over Pengower's most famous disk jockey: "He used to be on the local radio station before they went bust. You must remember him from back in the day. He had this great pop quiz —"

"Pop, crackle — snap!" Eben cried.

"Yes!" Alun cried. "That was it!" He cleared his throat and jiggled his head with pride. "I was actually a caller on your show once. I don't know if you remember…"

The former DJ was about to reply, when the journalist decided to interrupt: "Do people *really* still listen to the radio?"

"You surely must have listened to *Pen Wireless FM* when you were growing up," said Alun.

Rhiannon shook her head. "I think my Nain used to. Personally, I preferred curating my own choice of music growing up. That's what cassette tapes were for." She turned to the sad looking DJ. "Sorry… I guess you were just never on my radar. To be honest, I barely even knew we had a local radio station."

Her words seemed to cut the signalman deep into his chest, and he tried to hide his shock. "I think I must have had a slightly older demographic." He ignored Alun's cough. "People really loved tuning into my show."

"If that's the case," said Rhiannon, "then how did you find yourself manning a signal box?"

Eben shrugged. "This was just something I did on a Saturday. A little hobby of mine. I've been volunteering here for donkey's."

"And they let you sleep here?"

"Uh, no, actually." The disk jockey hung his head in shame. "Nobody else knows I'm here."

Alun and Rhiannon both looked at each other.

"It's only temporary," Eben continued. "I told the station master to put me down for more days. He thinks I've found another part-time job. He's a right clown. I don't know if you've met him?"

"Yes, we've met him."

The signalman's face darkened at the thought of his superior. "I'm the one who should have got that job. I've put in more hours than anyone at this place. Then old Sergeant Major walks in and just takes over." He looked up at his recording set-up and his mood lifted. "But none of that matters anymore. I've got my own radio station now."

Eben began moving around his dials, as the current song gradually faded out. He leant forward and hovered his lips around the microphone. "A little blast from the past there for all you loyal listeners," he announced. The tone of his voice had shifted to that of a professional airwave host. "It's a chilly evening out there, you lakeside dwellers, and DJ Bull is about to warm you up with another classic..."

Eben moved some more levers, and the song "The Heat Is On" by Glenn Frey came blasting out of the speakers. The proud disk jockey sat back in his chair again and turned to the intrigued members of his studio audience.

"Not a bad choice," said Rhiannon, tapping her foot.

"You should tune in," said Eben. "Always nice to welcome a new listener from the younger crowd."

Flattery will get you everywhere, Alun thought, as he noticed the pleased expression on his friend's face. "So, you record the whole show from this box?" he asked, looking around at the small space.

Eben nodded and stretched out his arms. "I've been thinking of calling the show: Live From The Hot Box!"

His two visitors didn't seem to share his enthusiasm.

"Maybe sleep on that one," said Rhiannon.

"My next step is sponsorship," said Eben. "It's where the last radio station went wrong. They kept losing their sponsors and relied on local advertising. I'm thinking of approaching the pyjama factory on the industrial estate. You know the one I mean?"

The two visitors turned to each other. "Oh, we know the one you mean. Good luck with that."

"It's not about luck," said the disk jockey, tapping the side of his head. "It's about good business sense. You don't achieve the success I have without a bit of strategy."

Rhiannon couldn't help but gaze around the room at the scattering of personal possessions and half-eaten takeaways. "Oh, we can see you definitely have *that*."

"Do you still take requests?" Alun asked.

"Of course! Name the song and it's yours."

The accountant felt a surge of excitement and began tickling his own chin in search of an artist.

"What was your relationship to Hefin Charles?" Rhiannon quickly asked.

Her question had caught the DJ off guard. "My relationship?"

"I assume you got to know the man whilst working here."

"We got on pretty well," said Eben. "But then he did with everyone. The man even let me sleep on the floor of his caravan when he found out I was staying here. I'd probably be there now if he hadn't died so suddenly. It just didn't seem right to keep sleeping there, like."

"He lived in a caravan?" Alun asked. The horrible flashbacks of a disastrous family holiday were coming back again.

"Oh, aye. He was pretty minimalist, old Hefin. Not big on

personal possessions. A bit of an old hippy, I suppose. Like me! The guy got his kicks from helping people. He said I was welcome to stay with him as long as I needed to get back on my feet again. I'll forever be grateful for that."

"Where's the caravan?" asked Rhiannon.

The signalman pointed to the north side of his box. "It's in a field over near the pub. The land belongs to a local farmer called Tecwyn. I think they had some arrangement going on."

"We met that farmer the other day," said Alun. "Small world."

"Yes," said Rhiannon. "A very small world. Sounds like this Hefin was a bit of a nomad, then."

"Aye," said Eben. "He might have had some gypsy blood in there somewhere. But he was from Aberystwyth, I think, originally. He settled here in Llanlyn just before his wife died. A long time ago now, though. They retired early and decided to spend the rest of their lives travelling around Wales, living out of their caravan. Quite romantic, I suppose."

Alun wasn't so sure he would have described living out the rest of his life in a caravan "romantic", but each to their own, he thought.

"Why did they settle in Llanlyn?" asked Rhiannon.

"He said it was the most beautiful place they had ever seen."

Alun couldn't have agreed more with *that* statement, on the other hand.

"Hefin and his wife became locals in their own right," Eben continued. "They were accepted by the community, and the rest was history."

"What a lovely story," said Rhiannon. "Shame about the gruesome ending."

The signalman nodded. "Yes, I suppose it is. Hefin's wife died of cancer in the end. And, well, we all know how *his* life ended."

All three of them went silent, mainly out of respect for the tragic deaths of this seemingly free-spirited couple. The Glenn Frey song continued to play out in the background and was a strange accompaniment to this solemn moment.

Alun and Rhiannon bid their farewells and left the man to his evening show. When they returned to the car, the accountant made a point of searching for it on his driver's radio.

"Aha!" He finished his tuning and sat back in his seat. "There it is."

Rhiannon glared at him, as Eben's radio voice could be heard throughout the vehicle. "You know I would normally kill a person for playing with my settings?"

Alun let out a nervous laugh and assumed she was joking.

They drove back through the village to the sound of "Club Tropicana" by Wham! It wasn't the first George Michael song that Rhiannon would have chosen to play at Christmas time, but she let it slide on this occasion.

"You didn't fancy offering him sponsorship yourself?" she asked, as they made their way back along the lake.

The accountant turned to see her mischievous smile. "I run a small business," he said, "not a charity. We're not making enough to just hand out to people."

Rhiannon winced. "Spoken like a true Scrooge. That was cold even for you."

"I can't sponsor a man who operates out of a signal box."

"You were acting like his biggest fan about ten minutes ago."

"That doesn't mean I have to give him money. I enjoy watching *The Weakest Link*. But I don't go paying extra on my TV licence."

"Whatever makes you feel less guilty."

Alun stared at the reflection of Pengower's street lights flickering on the lake. It had turned out that the sight of a man without a home for the night had really upset him. He would never wish that on anybody, and if he had possessed the additional finances to support him, he would have done so in an instant. The truth was, his business was only just supporting two salaries at that point in time, and he was already struggling to justify a Christmas party.

Rhiannon dropped her passenger back outside his house, and she called out to him through her car window. "I've been meaning to ask you something!" she cried. Alun was already half way up his garden path, and he turned around to head back. "What are you doing for Christmas Eve?"

Alun didn't even have to think. His day was very straightforward. "Nothing much," he said.

"Fancy coming to my parent's for dinner?"

"Oh, I wouldn't want to put anyone out."

Rhiannon placed her chin against the remaining glass on her rolled-down window. "*Please!* Don't make me suffer alone. You'd be doing me a huge favour. All my family are going to be there, and, well... *that's* enough to drive anyone crazy."

"Well," said Alun, "I'm sure I can manage it."

"Great!"

The journalist sped off before he had a chance to change his mind. She was keen to pick up her son and get back home. It had been a very long day, and an evening on the sofa was very much on the cards.

She pulled up outside her parent's house and made the dreaded walk to the front door. It wasn't easy dealing with her mother in such a tired mood. There was bound to be some sort of drama for her in just a few moments, whether it was her son's particular eating habits or an incident at the hairdresser's.

Rhiannon braced herself before pressing down on the doorbell. When the door eventually swung open, the person standing there to greet her was not who she had expected.

"Rhiannon!" the younger woman cried, pulling her in close for a tight squeeze.

The older sibling tried to act surprised and could smell the overpowering fragrance of a luxury perfume brand. She eventually felt the person's grip release, and Rhiannon saw the beaming smile of her younger sister.

"Hello, Awel."

CHAPTER 17

"You should have seen her face," said Awel Williams, pouring herself a glass of Prossecco. She gave her sister a mischievous smile. "I bet you didn't expect to see *me* at the door!"

Rhiannon cringed in the corner of her parent's living room. "Nope, I certainly did not. You weren't supposed to be here for a few more days."

"Well — surprise!" The younger sibling toasted her drink and giggled to herself. "And there's still another one to come..."

Her mother, Morwenna, swallowed the rest of her bubbly in one mouthful. "What do you mean, Awel?"

"Well..." Awel turned to the smug man dressed in a cartoonish Christmas jumper, and they both grinned like two lovestruck teenagers. "Do you want to tell them, or shall I?"

Morwenna gasped, as her daughter lifted up her finger to reveal an enormous ring. Rhiannon was equally as surprised, and the sound of her mother's scream pierced her ears.

"Awel! How could you keep that a secret from me?!" Morwenna leapt off her chair and began doing a little dance. "My little baby's getting married!"

Awel jumped up herself and joined her mother in a celebratory hug. Rhiannon forced out a big smile and was determined to remain in her seat.

"I'm going to be a Pratt!" Awel cried, holding back the tears.

Her sister couldn't help but laugh. That surname had aways tickled her. "I think in many ways," she said, "you've always been a Pratt at heart."

"Yeeeah," said Awel, turning to her future husband with a blush. It had not been the reaction Rhiannon had hoped for, and she tried not to vomit, as the two linked together for a kiss.

"Trust your father to not be here," said Morwenna. She looked at her watch and stomped her foot. "Where *is* that man?"

"You could have waited," Rhiannon muttered.

"He'd probably have a heart attack," said Gregory. "Weddings aren't cheap!"

Rhiannon turned to her future brother-in-law with a frown. "What makes you think he's paying for it?"

"Don't be daft, Rhiannon!" Awel glared at her. "The father of the bride *always* pays for the wedding."

"I'm sorry," said her sister. "I must have got stuck in the wrong century."

"It's about time that man splashed out a bit," said Morwenna, clutching her glass flute like an old friend. "The stingy sod."

Gregory Pratt sat himself down on the sofa and let his fiancé drop down onto his lap.

"Gregory proposed outside The Tate Modern," said Awel. "He's very cultured like that."

"Nice one, Greg."

Rhiannon's compliment was met with two frowns. The happy couple hated it when she called the man *Greg*. "He's not a pasty," Awel had previously told her.

"Have you thought about where you'd like the wedding?" Morwenna asked.

Awel somehow managed to become more giddy than she already was. "Actually, we're thinking of having the wedding here — in Pengower!"

Her mother screeched for the second time that evening. "This is so exciting! Wait until I tell the girls. Oh! We could have the reception over at the golf club!"

"You'd better start looking for a bridesmaid dress," said Gregory, shooting a sly grin towards his future sister-in-law.

"Oh, yes!" Awel clapped her hands. "Rhiannon, you're going to be my bridesmaid! Isn't that exciting?"

Rhiannon could feel her body trembling in terror. "Yes... so exciting..."

"We can all do a little shop together," said Morwenna. "Have a proper girly afternoon."

"It just keeps getting better," Rhiannon muttered.

"I know! What a special Christmas this is!"

"Enough about us," said Awel, still nestled in her fiancé's arms. "How are things with you, Rhiannon?"

Her sister was mid-gulp on the Prosecco and gave it a painful swallow. "Oh, just the usual. You know, same old."

"How are you adjusting to life as a country bumpkin?" asked Gregory with a smirk. "Never imagined *you* settling down in a place like this."

"It's growing on me," said Rhiannon. "How's the — wait, what is it you do again?"

"He's a television executive," Awel snapped. "I've told you about this before."

"Oh, that's right. You work on that reality TV show with bratty, rich kids."

"It's *called Sloanies*! It won two awards last year. *And* it's been commissioned for another series."

"Never watched it."

"It's alright," said Gregory, rubbing his fiancé on the shoulder. "Documentaries aren't everybody's thing."

"Documentary?" asked Rhiannon. "We're calling *Sloanies* a documentary now?"

"Rhiannon!" Morwenna shouted. "For what it's worth, I absolutely *love* your programme, Gregory. I've watched every single episode." She gave her disgruntled, future son-in-law a cheerful wave.

That made a lot of sense, Rhiannon thought. Her mother was the perfect target audience for a programme about people sat around in trendy bars sipping on cocktails.

"How's your work going?" Gregory asked. "Still working in tabloids?"

"Not anymore," said Rhiannon. "I'm working for an independent press here in North Wales."

"It's this one," said Morwenna, chucking him a dated copy of *The Merioneth Press* from the coffee table.

"It's a little, local paper," said Awel.

"That must be why I've never heard of it," said Gregory, savouring his moment of sweet revenge. He flicked through the pages and laughed at one of the headlines. "Farmer falls into slurry?!"

"That's an old one," Rhiannon muttered. "Not one of mine."

"So, come on, sis," said Awel. "Any future husbands for you on the horizon?"

Morwenna cackled. "Chance would be a fine thing." A sudden thought caused her to frown. "Although, I can't be doing with *two* weddings to organise!"

"You don't need to worry about that, mother." Rhiannon saw the row of curious eyes on her and wanted to hide behind the sofa. "I'm not seeing anyone."

"Aw," said Awel. "That's a shame." She turned to her partner. "Hey! We should introduce her to Stewart!"

"Stewart?" Gregory asked. "You think Steward would be —"

"It's alright," Rhiannon interrupted. "You don't need to set me up. I'm not even looking."

"What about that nice, young accountant?" Morwenna asked, knowing she was going to get a reaction.

"Mam!" her daughter cried. "I've told you — Alun and I are just friends."

"Accountant, eh?" Gregory began nudging his fiance who tried not to laugh. "Not a bad choice that, Rhiannon."

"Leave her alone!" Awel cried. "She's been through a lot, Rhiannon has. It can't be easy having the life she has. What with the divorce... and the single-mother thing."

"Oh, you're so sweet, love." Morwenna gave her youngest daughter a proud tap on the knee.

"She's the best!" Gregory chimed in.

"Yeah," said Rhiannon. "She's great."

The journalist left her parent's house wanting to gasp at the air outside. It was like someone had trapped her in a box with no oxygen, and now she could finally breathe.

She clutched Gwyl's hand and walked him to the front gate. The three-year-old continued to tell his mother how much fun his Auntie Awel and Uncle Gregory were, all the way until they reached the car.

Rhiannon sat in the driver seat and longed for something to take her mind off the day's events. She fired up the engine and heard the familiar voice of a local DJ coming from the radio. Her jaw began to swing from side to side, grinding her clenched set of teeth.

"This is your friend DJ Bull coming to you live on this frosty evening beside Pengower Lake. A shout out to all you lonely hearts out there who need a bit of cheering up this Christmas. I've got just the ticket..."

The opening bars of "Lonely This Christmas" by Mud filled the entire car, as it sped away from the quiet cul-de-sac.

CHAPTER 18

Rhiannon heard another rumble underneath her car. The dirt road leading to Talardd Farm had touched the bottom of the Renault Scenic four times since coming off the main road, and the vehicle's owner knew that there was only so much punishment it could take.

"Not another one!" she cried at the sight of another gate. The journalist sighed and turned to her assistant. "Sorry, George."

The intern took the hint and climbed out. His driver watched him stumble over a series of puddles until he reached the gate. After letting the car through, he returned to his seat with his favourite trainers covered in mud.

"Do we really need to visit Tecwyn's farm?" he asked, as they continued to crawl along the bumpy road.

"I'd say that the only person to use that crossing every day must know *something*," said Rhiannon.

"He's not the most approachable person," said George, kicking off pieces of mud.

"I gathered that from the other day. I suppose anyone who lives this remote isn't exactly going to be the most sociable butterfly."

George shrugged. "Farmers around here tend to be quite friendly usually."

"What makes you say that?"

"I see a lot of them at the young farmers club in the village."

"You go to a *young farmers* club?" Rhiannon asked.

The intern blushed. "It's not just for farmers. Everybody goes. All the young people, anyway."

"Sounds like you're a bit of a dark horse."

They passed a stretch of empty fields before approaching a white farmhouse with a green barn. There was no sign of life for miles around, and the edge of Pengower Lake could be seen up in the distance.

"Finally," said Rhiannon. "No more gates."

George could not have agreed more, especially seeing as he was the one who had to open them all. But the journalist had spoken a little too soon, and there was still one last gate before they could drive through into the yard.

"He'd better be home," said Rhiannon, as she climbed out of the vehicle to greet her muddy intern. "I think it's probably better that you stay in the car." George hung his head in disappointment. "No offence, but it's hard for me to put the pressure on when I'm standing beside —"

"It's okay," George said. "I understand."

He climbed back into the car, and the journalist felt a wave of guilt. She knew what it was like to be young and keen — even after becoming older and more reluctant.

The farm appeared to be in a much better condition than many of the other farms she'd visited (and since moving back to Pengower, she'd seen a few). Its barn was spotless, and the tractor sitting inside was sparkling clean. Even the ground had been tidied up with a layer of hard gravel, and there wasn't a piece of scrap or rubbish in sight.

When she reached the front door, the sound of barking sheep dogs made her jump.

"Can I help you?" asked the suspicious woman in the open doorway.

"Maybe," said Rhiannon. "Is Tecwyn around?"

Ruth McNaught, the wife of Tecwyn McNaught, studied the woman's face.

"What do you want with him?" she asked. "You're like these tradesmen who always want to speak with my husband instead of me — like I'm some helpless, little damsel. Well, this is my farm as much as his."

"Oh, don't worry, I get it." Rhiannon held up her hands. "Single mother over here."

The woman wanted to lower her guard but reminded herself not to be so gullible.

"If you're selling something," she said, "we ain't buying."

"I'm definitely not selling. I work for the local newspaper."

"Then we're definitely not interested. Last time we spoke to your lot, they tricked us into some 'Neighbours from hell' article."

The journalist was not the least bit surprised. "That must have been before my time."

Ruth gave her a dry smile. "Make sure you close the gates on your way out." She was about to slam the door shut, when the sight of another stranger on her property caused her to hesitate. "Wait," she said, squinting towards the other side of the yard. "Is that George-Shop?"

Rhiannon turned around to find her intern leaning against a fence with a long zoom lens. "I'm sorry about him. I asked him to stay in the —"

"You're here with George-Shop?" asked Ruth. The other woman nodded, and she stepped aside. "I guess you'd both better come in."

A surprised Rhiannon began frantically trying to wave down her intern and signalled for him to come over. George was surprised at the sudden burst of enthusiasm but was pleased to be needed.

The inside of Talardd Farm was as tidy as the outside. Every kitchen utensil seemed to be in its proper place and each surface had been kept clear.

"You run a tight ship," said Rhiannon, as the sound of the kettle boiling warmed her soul.

Ruth dripped some excess milk against the kitchen counter and hurried to wipe it down. "That's my doing," she said. "Mess is stress, as my dad used to say. If I had it my way, we'd be spreading our fields with soap, not silage."

"You remind me of someone else I know. Personally, I'm a bit of a slob."

"My husband used to be. But we sorted that right out early on."

Rhiannon listened in disbelief, as the woman went on to describe the various techniques she used to train her other-half. She had thought Marie Kondo was bonkers, and, now, there was Ruth McNaught. She was also surprised that her partner was the exact same person who had shouted a series of expletives from his Land Rover window that day at the crossing. He hadn't exactly struck her as a hen-pecked husband.

"Where is your husband now?" she asked.

"He's out there fixing one of the fences," said Ruth. "Although he's been gone all morning. It's a fence, not the Berlin Wall. He's either getting slow or just incompetent. Probably both."

Rhiannon didn't blame Tecwyn for taking his time. She wouldn't want to rush home to face the wrath of his wife either. Ruth McNaught was quite an intimidating person for her size and didn't seem like the type to suffer fools.

"Why exactly do you need to see my husband, anyway?" Ruth asked. "He's the most boring man on the planet. There can't be anything he's got to say that a newspaper would want to print.

"Did you say that you've already had dealings with the press already?" Rhiannon asked back.

Ruth snarled and brought over their hot drinks. "That little rat over at Deryn Farm went to the papers after we reported him to the police."

"That's Wali Henryd, isn't it?" asked George, who was grateful for the plate of biscuits.

"Wolly Henryd, more like!" Ruth lifted up a sharp kitchen knife which alarmed her two visitors. "Anyone for cake?" She then offered up a Victoria sponge in her other hand. They both declined. "Anyway, the man's been a nuisance for years: fly tipping on our land, stealing our sheep, spreading viruses... the guy's a complete crackpot. We're talking about a man who claims to have seen aliens."

George couldn't help but smile. He knew about Wali and had heard all the stories. The man had even featured on an obscure television program about UFO sightings. He had provided the school playground at Llanlyn with a wealth of gossip and tall tales. Many of them were the product of young imaginations and some were probably true.

"Why didn't you report him to the police sooner?" asked Rhiannon.

"We never had any proof. It wasn't until he was stupid enough to shoot one of our sheep that we knew we'd have him. But when he didn't get charged, the man went straight to the press — told them all these crazy, made-up lies about us — and they believed him! They sent a reporter to get our side of the story and just ignored it. These journalists have no shame."

Rhiannon coughed. "We're not all bad," she said.

"Well, then maybe you can write a new article about an alien-hugging lunatic who torments his fellow farmers." Ruth crossed her arms and shook her head. "If you can even call him a farmer."

"I'd love to," said Rhiannon, "but it's not really in my brief. I'm more interested in —" A sudden thought popped into her head. "Wait, wait, wait... did you say he shot your sheep?"

"The sick fool," said Ruth. "He shouldn't be allowed anywhere near animals."

"So he owns a firearm?"

"We're farmers. Most of us at least have an old rifle in the shed, even if we never use one. But Wali probably owns a laser gun, knowing him."

The journalist smiled. "Maybe there's a way to get your own back on this Wali." She had acquired the woman's full attention. "Do you think he's capable of murder?"

Ruth scoffed. "He's definitely a sheep murderer. Why?"

Rhiannon pulled out her notepad with a pen at the ready. "Tell me everything about this Wali Henryd. All the dirt you have."

The two visitors from *The Merioneth Press* remained in the kitchen of Talardd Farm for another whole hour. They listened, as Ruth McNaught took pleasure in divulging every last detail of their dealings with the neighbouring farm and its unusual owner.

By the time they had left the house and bid their farewells, George's head was a spinning mess. Rhiannon, on the other hand, had heard a lot worse and had come to the early conclusion that Wali Henryd was indeed a "crackpot". She also knew that even crackpots could be dangerous and decided it was time to pay another farm a visit.

The two visitors returned to their car and, with the doors slammed firmly shut, they were able to speak freely.

"Do you really think Wali Henryd killed Hefin Charles?" asked George. "He doesn't seem the type."

Rhiannon shrugged. "Nobody ever does. But it's our first hint of a firearm, so it's worth a look. Maybe he mistook Hefin as a hostile, red alien?"

"Or a sheep," said the intern.

"Or a sheep..."

The sound of a loud bang against the windscreen caused them both to jump. They looked up to see a furious Tecwyn with his hand against the glass.

"What do you think you're doing?" the muffled voice cried.

Rhiannon wound her window down. "Sorry, I didn't catch that."

The farmer went red. "I said —"

"Yes, we heard you the first time. Do you mind not touching my car?"

"You're on my property!" Tecwyn roared.

The journalist looked around the yard in feigned surprise. "And a very nice one it is too." She winked at him with a sly grin. "We were just talking to your wife, actually. She makes a lovely cuppa."

The farmer went pale. "You did — what?"

"She didn't seem very happy, though, mind you."

"She *didn't*?"

Rhiannon was taking great pleasure in making the man sweat. Everybody had their Achilles heel, and Tecwyn McNaught's greatest trigger point was his wife.

She made gentle tutting sounds which only sucked the man in even more. "Sounds like you're really in the doghouse this time."

"What for?" Tecwyn asked, defending himself like a scalded schoolboy.

"It's not my place to say," Rhiannon whispered. "Just tread

lightly. You should probably get inside before she gets any worse."

Tecwyn looked up towards the farmhouse and seemed nervous to make the move. The car fired up and Rhiannon paused before taking off the handbrake. "Oh," she called across the engine noise, "I wanted to ask you something." The farmer was more preoccupied with what horrors might be waiting for him inside. "Is it true that you own a field near the village? The one with Hefin Charles' caravan on it?"

Now Tecwyn's focus was very quickly back on the reporter. "Who told you that?"

"Is it true?"

"Yeah, it's my field. What about it?" He crouched down and lowered his head down to the height of the window. "Who did you say you are again?"

"Sorry, must dash!"

Rhiannon's car almost reversed over the man's foot had he not moved in time. Soon, the Renault Scenic was bumping its way back across the dirt road. When it reached the first gate, the car made a sudden stop, and George was confused to hear his driver turn off the engine. She climbed out of the vehicle and began peering off into the distance.

"What's the matter?" asked the intern, who was keen to get moving.

Rhiannon pointed in the opposite direction of Talardd Farm, towards something on the other side of a narrow river. "That must be it over there," she said. "Deryn Farm, the home of that Wali man."

George squinted with his naturally poor eyesight. He could have done with the help of his trusty zoom lens. "Yes, I suppose it is. How did you know that?"

"I checked the map before we came. Do you youngsters know what a map is? Or is it all satellite images these days?"

The intern didn't even have a chance to respond, as he watched her walk away in disbelief.

Rhiannon headed towards the river and prepared to roll up her trousers. "Are you coming or what?"

"What about the car?" George called out.

"We don't need that. We're taking a shortcut!"

CHAPTER 19

The river was shallow but cold. In the words of *The Merioneth Press'* latest intern, it was "absolutely freezing!".

"Hurry up then!" Rhiannon called out from the other side of the water. Her trousers were still rolled up above her knees, and the pair of boots in her hand had narrowly avoided a good soaking. "The longer you stand there, the colder you'll get!"

George did his best to ignore the concerns of impending hypothermia and continued to wade his way across the river. The local young man knew these waters well, and he also knew better than to try and take a dip in them during the middle of winter. But his colleague had been adamant that they were quicker hiking to the next farm than they were driving all the way around. She also explained about the important element of "surprise". You never knew what a person might be getting up to when nobody else was around, especially a person like Wali Henryd. To catch him in the act of something truly despicable or unlawful would have only made their investigation easier.

"Where's your other sock?" Rhiannon asked, as she helped to pull her bare-footed photographer up onto the bank.

George turned around and saw his lonely sock resting against the shore on the other side of the river. "I guess I'll have to get it on the way back," he said with a heavy heart.

They traipsed across the frosty grassland, until the outbuildings of Deryn Farm had grown in size. Eventually, the two hikers were close enough to hear a dog barking, something that alarmed the intern.

"Are you sure this is a good idea?" asked George.

Rhiannon didn't answer and signalled for him to follow her towards the back of the property.

Unbeknownst to his creeping visitors, Wali Henryd was holding up a double-barrelled shotgun and bracing himself for impact. He honed in on his target, closed his eyes and, with all the willpower of a ruthless hunter, he pulled the trigger.

The blast was deafening. With a weary face, the farmer with the enormous bushy beard opened his eyes again to observe the damage.

In the corner of his barn was a small bunker with a metallic exterior. Wali headed over to this futuristic looking cabin and inspected the bullet holes. He swung open the screaming door and was disappointed to find that the bullets had travelled straight through into the back of the bunker.

"Damn it!" he cried. The farmer slammed the flimsy door shut and waited for the echo to pass. In the silent aftermath Wali heard something that made him freeze. Someone was watching him, he thought. Without the slightest hesitation, he turned around and lifted up his rifle.

The two strangers on the other side of the yard raised their arms up in fright.

"Don't shoot!" George cried, staring down the barrel of a shotgun. He was positioned behind a pile of old crates, somewhere his colleague had insisted they hide behind. After a restrained cough (probably caused by the impromptu dip in that freezing cold river), their cover was blown.

"We come in peace," said Rhiannon, lifting up her fingers like a crew member from *Star Trek*. Wali let out a short grunt and lowered his weapon. "You nearly ended up looking like that door!" he cried. Rhiannon and George glanced at the sea of bullet holes and gulped. "You scared the life out of me!"

"Oh, I'm sorry." Rhiannon turned to her colleague with a cynical frown. She had barely recovered from having a shotgun pointed at her. "The last thing we wanted to do was scare you. How careless of us..."

"Apology accepted!" Wali cried. "You can't be too careful these days. It's good to keep your wits about you." He pointed to the pile of broken crates in front of them. "I wouldn't stand too close to all that. I found a nest in there last week."

The journalist didn't need telling twice, and she swiftly stepped away from her hiding spot. The man hadn't mentioned exactly what type of nest he had supposedly found, but Rhiannon did not want to take her chances. Any animal with a nest was usually one she didn't want to be around.

"Is there a particular reason that you're going to war with a tin shed?" she asked.

The farmer let out a manic laugh. "Tin shed!" He turned to the young man beside her, who also wasn't keen on getting too close to the nest. "She's funny, your friend." Wali straightened his wonky pair of glasses. "You're Ela-Shop's son, aren't you?" George nodded. "I thought so. I was only just talking to her the other day about her milk. You've got to watch where you get milk from nowadays. I read this article on how the government have been taking over the big dairy suppliers so they can inject us with these formulas. Think about it — what food source does the population consume the most? Milk! They can get access to us even when we're pouring our morning cereals!"

"I wouldn't know about all that," said George. "I'm lactose intolerant."

"When you say *article*," said Rhiannon with a cynical frown, "you must mean — social media post?"

"Social media?!" Wali cried. "I wouldn't be caught dead going on Facetime or Whatsup and all that rubbish." He began tapping a grubby finger against the side of his head. "No, that's *really* how they brainwash you. I don't even have a mobile phone. I'm completely off the grid!"

He was completely off his *something*, Rhiannon thought to herself. "Then how, if you don't mind me asking, do you hear about these stories like your milk conspiracy?"

"Mind?" asked Wali. He dropped his gun to the floor (much to the relief of his visitors) and marched over to her with a wild expression. "I don't mind at all! In fact, I'm quite happy to tell you!"

Rhiannon was starting to seriously regret her question, and she could smell the man's body odour as he came closer. It seemed that Wali Henryd was a man who loved to ramble and wasn't used to people taking an interest in his favourite topics.

Like a scruffy magician, the man pulled out a rolled up magazine from the inside of his jacket. "I've got a subscription, see. Most people would never think to do this, which is exactly why the general public are so clueless. But this publication has all the latest intel on what's *really* going on in this world."

The journalist scanned the cover. "It's dated February last year..."

"Uh, yes. That's because it's produced over in America. By the time it gets over here, we're normally a little behind."

"America?" Rhiannon asked, studying the cover's image of a

large complex in the middle of the desert. "Well, it's a good job the Americans are on top of the Welsh dairy industry."

"That's it, you see!" Wali looked up towards the sky, causing the two people opposite to do the same. "It's all happening on a global scale."

George stared up at the gaggle of geese going past above their heads. "You mean, like global warming?"

"Global warming," the farmer repeated in a more dismissive tone. "Global warming is just a distraction. They want us to be more concerned about the weather than the *real* threat."

"Let me guess," said Rhiannon, who was still watching the sky. "A hostile alien takeover?"

"No!" Wali cried. "Well, at least not yet." His face was so close to Rhiannon's that she could smell his breath. "We're talking about a threat down here on our very own planet — from the people who collect our waste, supply our food, control our gas and electric…"

"Are you telling me that my utility provider is secretly planning on invading my house?" Rhiannon tutted. "No wonder their customer support line keeps me on hold for so long."

"Think about it — they have the power to take away all our basic needs. They have us over a barrel. We've become too dependent on them, and now they know it!"

"Even *Scottish Power*?"

"Especially *Scottish Power*! Are we anywhere near Scotland right now? I don't think so."

Rhiannon had heard more than enough, and she decided to walk towards the barn to get some fresh air. "This is all fascinating," she said, pointing towards the metal bunker. "But what does all this have to do with *that* monstrosity?"

Wali turned to his handmade shelter with a surge of pride. "I need to be prepared for the inevitable — for when the Controllers decide to turn on us."

"The *Controllers*?" asked George. The young man had become fully invested in the farmer's story. Whether he believed it all was yet to be decided, but, at least from his perspective, Wali seemed to make a good point.

"The *Controllers!*" cried Wali, waving his magazine. "It's a technical term for the people at the top, the people who have the power to take over."

"Like the council?" asked the intern.

"*Especially* the council!" the farmer cried, placing a hand on his shoulder. He could sense when a person was on board and young George seemed to be making his way up the gangway.

"But if they take us over... who will run the public services for *them*?"

Wali scratched his head. The young man's question had almost stumped him. "Well," he said, "the *Controllers* will need to set up a new council. Like we have now."

The young photographer wanted to ask if perhaps "the Controllers" had already taken over and that the current council was just the new one. But, then again, what did *he* know about these things?

"And what are these for?" asked Rhiannon, pointing at the bullet marks scattered across the bunker. "Air holes?"

Wali blushed. "Uh, not quite. I was just testing its durability."

"Against a machine gun?!"

"The Controllers will use as much force as is necessary, especially when they have an entire police force at their disposal."

"No offence to your magazine," said Rhiannon, whilst snooping around inside the shelter. "But our police is a little different to the one in the states. I'd be more worried about a bombardment of truncheons." She took one last look at the pile of supplies (consisting mainly of a single blanket and an excessive amount of baked bean cans) and walked back outside to the smell of freedom. "I suppose you probably want to know why we're here?"

The farmer took off his glasses and used them to scratch his head. "I suppose so," he said, having secretly not even asked himself the question.

"We've just been visiting your lovely neighbours," Rhiannon continued. "You probably know them. The McNaughts?"

Wali's face darkened. "Yes, I know them."

"They spoke very highly of you."

The farmer couldn't have looked more surprised. "Did they?"

"No, not really."

"Oh..." Wali hung his head in disappointment. "I wouldn't pay much attention to anything that they've got to say. They're a bunch of lying crooks."

Rhiannon tried to close the bunker door and failed miserably. The sheet of metal was so battered that it was barely hanging on by its hinges. "Funny you should say that. Because they said similar things about you. Which surprises me given that you seem like just a normal guy."

Wali scoffed. "They're just bitter about the fact that I took back some of their land — land which is rightfully mine!" He noticed the woman's surprise and smiled. "I bet they didn't mention that part!"

"No," Rhiannon muttered, annoyed that she had lost the upper hand. "They didn't."

"This farm, this land — it's been in my family for generations. I was born in that very spot!"

Rhiannon and George followed his pointed finger and couldn't work out whether he meant the farmhouse or the nearby pigsty. They hoped it wasn't the latter.

"Then this couple come along and buy Talardd Farm, acting like they own everything. *Madarchs* we call them around here!"

"Excuse me?" asked Rhiannon.

"Madarchs! People who aren't born into a farm's legacy. Their DNA isn't ingrained through the soil — their forefathers didn't toil away so that they could have the right to farm."

"You sound like a member of the landed gentry." She looked around the yard full of mysterious pieces of junk and piles of rubbish. It was a far cry from the property she had just visited. "And yet there's nothing posh about this place."

Wali shrugged. "I just believe in owning what's rightfully yours."

"How much land did you claim back from them, exactly?"

The farmer let out a proud grin. "All in all, it was about a couple of acres. Which is only a slither as far as they're concerned. But that's not the point! Every blade of grass is precious in my book."

"Clearly," said Rhiannon, looking over at three disused washing machines dumped in the nearby field.

"I went through a lot of trouble to get that land back. I rooted through all of the family deeds and paperwork. I even hired a solicitor! Now that was a new frontier, I can tell you."

They were both distracted by the camera pointing in their direction. George was in full snapshot-mode and had already been scurrying around the yard taking photos.

"Hey!" Wali cried before approaching the young man with an excited smile. "If you want something interesting to photograph, I can show you a few things, lad!" He went serious for a moment. "You're not allergic to asbestos, are you?"

Before the intern could answer, Rhiannon jumped in to interrupt. "Before you do that," she said, lifting up an old map she had acquired during her research of the area. "Would you mind highlighting this extra bit land for me?"

Wali pushed up his glasses and took the red marker from her. With his tongue sticking out from the side of his mouth, he began marking off a section of the map.

Rhiannon stared at the red marks with a satisfied smile. "That's perfect," she said. "Just perfect."

CHAPTER 20

"**D**o you think there are enough sausage rolls?" asked Alun in a panic. He had never been so stressed in all of his life and was seriously considering taking off his Christmas jumper.

"I'd be more worried about the fizz," said Ffion, who was standing beside him, as they overlooked the office. "People come to these things for the free booze, not the sausage rolls."

The room was almost completely unrecognisable from its usual, orderly appearance. Its plain and clinical feel had been livened up by an explosion of colour and decorations. A huge buffet of food and drink had been meticulously laid out in front of the tax return filing cabinets, and next door to the photo-copier was an entire sound board with a pair giant speakers on the other side. This professional disco set-up, complete with strobe lighting and a dance floor, even had its own host — the one and only — DJ Bull.

The moonlighting radio host (and part-time signalman) connected his last power plug and gave his new client the thumbs-up. Alun returned the gesture with a thumbs-up of his own and caused Ffion to giggle into her pre-party drink. It was as though the junior accountant's boss had been beamed up by an unidentified flying object and replaced with Father Christmas himself.

"You mean, people don't come to these parties to celebrate the spirit of Christmas?"

Ffion turned to check if the man's question was sincere (if it was, then someone must have indeed spiked his coffee with magical fairy dust, after all). "Oh," she said, raising up her glass of gin with a wink. "they definitely come along for the *spirits*."

"God, you're right!" Alun cried, pacing the room like someone in a maternity ward. "What if we run out of sparkling?"

"Are you alright?" asked Ffion. "You seem a bit stressed."

The apprentice could not have been more on the money: Alun *was* stressed. *Very* stressed. It had taken a lot of time and research to put this work Christmas party together, and he wasn't prepared to let a shortage of bubbly ruin everything.

"I'm fine," he said, still pacing. "Just wondering where everyone is, that's all. I sent out all the invites and made it very clear that it starts at six — sharp."

They both looked up at the clock to see that it was already ten minutes past six.

"Relax," said Ffion. "People will come." Her tone was not as assured as she had intended it to be. "And if they don't, so what?!" She handed her boss a drink. "At least we, the work-force, are all here. That's all that really matters. At least *we* can celebrate."

Alun could see the genuine enthusiasm in her eyes and he smiled. "I suppose you're right."

They clinked their glasses together and laughed.

"Here he is!" cried a voice from the open doorway. "The man in charge!"

The accountant felt his enthusiasm dwindle, as Ffion's boyfriend, Neil, swanned into the room whilst puffing out his chest. The man joined the only other partygoers in the room and shook Alun's hand.

"Cool party, Al! This place is jumping."

He turned to his girlfriend with a smirk but didn't receive one in return. Instead, he had to settle for a cold glare.

"I thought you said you weren't fussed about coming," said Ffion.

"You know me," said Neil, placing his arm around her. "I've never been one to miss out on free beer."

"You should find some on that table, over there," said Alun. "It's mainly wine, though, so hopefully we have enough."

"I'll be the judge of that." Neil let out a mischievous chuckle. "Thank you kindly, governor!"

The disappointed accountant turned to his only employee. "Well, I guess that's it, then. Nobody else is coming."

Ffion was struggling to come up with some comforting words, when two new people appeared in the doorway. The sight of them both filled her boss with joy.

"Sorry we're late," said Rhiannon. Her boots were still muddy from the impromptu hike, and the intern by her side was even more dishevelled than she was. "We had to make a quick detour."

Alun rushed over to hug them both. The journalist and her assistant were a little taken aback by the unexpected enthusiasm (and unusual physical contact) but put it all down to alcohol and a dash of Christmas spirit.

"So glad you could make it," said Alun, taking their coats and escorting them over to the buffet table. "Help yourself to anything you want."

Rhiannon couldn't have been happier with the offer of some much needed sustenance, especially after a day in the great outdoors, and, yet, her friend's spitting resemblance to an enlightened Ebenezer Scrooge at the end of A Christmas Carol was still a concern. At least he wasn't in his pyjamas, she thought.

The accountant looked around at the four party members and was surprisingly satisfied. "What more could you ask for?" he asked with a raise of his glass. "I think this is the best party I've ever attended!"

Although Alun had attended very few parties in his time (the last one having featured two murders at a country estate), he wasn't prepared to disclose that fact on this occasion.

"Couldn't agree more," said Rhiannon. "Who needs a crowd of freeloaders to mingle with when you're surrounded by friends?"

She raised her glass, and the others joined in.

"You see," said Ffion, smiling at her boss. "I told you this was a good idea."

Neil was busy stuffing his face over at the buffet table. He swallowed his last mouthful, grabbed his drink and joined his girlfriend, as she completed the toast.

"You guys are joking, right?" The man looked around the room with his nose raised. "There's hardly anyone here. If it doesn't liven up soon, we might have to grab a few at the *Bull's Head*."

"Neil!" Ffion snapped. "Stop being rude."

The rest of the room performed an awkward pause, until Alun clapped his hands together in an attempt to lighten the mood. "Hey! I know what we need!" He scurried over to their makeshift DJ booth. "We need a bit of *Shaky*!"

Eben did the honours and fired up the song "Merry Christmas Everyone" by Shakin' Stevens.

"Now we're talking!" Rhiannon cried, making her way over to the dance floor whilst dragging her reluctant intern.

Neil erupted with laughter and spilled some of his beer. "Not *this* song! Where's all the banging tunes?"

Ffion shot him a furious scowl but it didn't seem to discourage him.

"You coming?" Neil asked her, grabbing his coat.

His girlfriend turned around to look at the other three bobbing around nearby. "Actually... I think I'm going to stay."

A surprised Neil saw the reluctance in her face and chuckled. "Suit yourself," he said. "You know where to find me when you get bored."

He gave the room a quick salute and marched off. As he disappeared through the doorway, a latecomer took his place. A confused farmer with a carrier bag of bitter removed his flat cap.

"Mr Nant!" Alun called out. "You made it!"

His local client caught his wave and scratched his own head. "Is this the right place?"

More popular Christmas songs were blasted out across the office, and over the next few hours, the small group of party-goers indulged their way through the large selection of food and drink.

Alun and Rhiannon had eventually found themselves slumped beside each other on a pair of office chairs. Their heads were already throbbing, and they watched in awe and wonder at the pair of younger individuals still bouncing around on the dance floor.

It had turned out that George was quite the dancer after a glass or two of social lubricant and was currently the life and soul of the party (at least, as far as *he* was concerned). His talent for busting out a few moves when the opportunity arose was something he attributed to his mother's obsession with Fred Astaire musicals.

"How are they still going?" asked Rhiannon, whilst slurring her words and rubbing her forehead. "We're not that old, are we?"

Alun turned to her with his drooping eyelids. "I guess you're as young as you behave," he replied.

"Wow. Then you must be pushing ninety, Alun Hughes." Rhiannon waited for him to react with the obligatory frown and giggled. "Only kidding!" She patted him on the back. "You've done alright tonight, to be fair. I didn't think you had it in you to arrange a party."

"Neither did I," said Alun. "It's a lot harder than it looks. But, I suppose, if there's ever a time to try something new, it's Christmas."

He turned his drunken face to see that Rhiannon was staring at him. For a moment, he wondered if it was the Christmas hat dangling from his head or the red stains across his teeth from the sherry, but then he realised she was just staring. Their heads began to move closer together, like there was some kind of magnetic pull trying to get them both to touch.

Just at the verge of impact, the moment was shattered by a call coming from the dance floor.

"Rhiannon! Rhiannon!!" George was jumping up and down whilst pointing towards speakers. The opening to "Galway Girl" by Ed Sheeran sent the young man into a dizzy frenzy.

"Is he alright?" asked Alun, having been broken away from the powerful spell.

Rhiannon rolled her eyes. "This must be Ed Sheeran," she muttered. "George is a big fan. As you can see."

Ffion seemed to be the only person impressed by the intern's burst of excitement and did her best to keep up.

"You like Ed Sheeran?" she called out to him.

"I *love* Ed Sheeran!" George cried back before pulling her into a playful jig.

"Should we tell him to slow down on the fizz?" Alun asked, as they continued to watch him from the other side of the room.

"He's a big boy," said Rhiannon. "I'm sure he knows his

limits." Her words sounded a lot more convinced than she really was, and the young man's manic singing was certainly a cause for concern.

"So how many farms did you say that you visited today?" Alun asked.

"Just two," Rhiannon muttered, noticing some more dirt marks on her trousers. "And two's more than enough for anyone."

The accountant pondered. "It makes things so much harder." He paused and saw his friend waiting for him to elaborate. "The gunshot, I mean. It means anyone could have done it. Without knowing the gun type, they could have been a whole mile away."

"A bullet can travel as far as a mile?"

"I've no idea. This is the problem. And with it being such an open area, I doubt anyone would have noticed the gunshot."

"Did I tell you about the yellow man?"

Alun turned to her with an intrigued expression. Rhiannon proceeded to tell him about the mysterious stranger in the hooded yellow raincoat. He was more surprised by the woman who spied on her long-distance neighbours with a pair of binoculars, but they would have to discuss that another time.

"Could just be a local walker," he eventually said.

"How many times have you taken a shovel with you on a walk?"

She had a point. "We did see some patches of disturbed ground," he said.

"And I doubt that there were *two* people out there digging that day."

Alun turned his mind to the two farms: a classic tale of disputed land and neighbourly feuds. He didn't doubt that the two despised each other, but whether any of it involved Hefin Charles was anyone's guess.

"Oh," said Rhiannon. "There's one more thing." She fetched

her handbag and showed him the dirtied map. "So, the land that they were fighting over is right here —"

Alun stared at the small outline. "That's the field Hefin's caravan's on."

"Yup!" Rhiannon grinned. She loved finding a link.

"Oi!!!"

Alun and Rhiannon both looked up to see a furious Neil standing in the doorway. George and Ffion were still dancing to the songs of Ed Sheeran, but now they had fully embraced each other to perform a jive.

"Get your hands off her!" Neil cried again. The man had clearly consumed a few pints in the time he had been away, and he began stomping his way across the room with eyes fixated firmly on the startled intern.

"Neil!" Ffion cried. "What are you playing at?"

Her words did little to discourage her boyfriend's furious advances, and, soon, he was grabbing George by the collar and forcing him into a chokehold.

"Neil! No!!"

Before Alun and Rhiannon could even climb to their feet, Eben vaulted over the DJ table and went charging towards Neil like an enraged rhinoceros. The big-boned man collided with his target and sent them both flying to the ground with a vicious tackle.

Having been released from the clutches of his attacker, George had sobered up very quickly and was still trying to make sense of what was happening. "We were just dancing!" he cried at the man who was now being pinned down by the heroic DJ.

Alun and Rhiannon joined the commotion taking place on the dance floor and found Ffion in tears. "I'm so sorry," she said. "He's never like this. It's all just a misunderstanding!"

"Get off!" Neil roared, gasping for air underneath the heavy weight.

"It's alright!" Eben called out to the rest of the room. "I used to be on the Pengower rugby team. This stuff used to happen all the time."

Rhiannon watched the upbeat DJ struggling away on the floor and spoke her thoughts: "Who knew? Bull by name, bull by nature."

CHAPTER 21

Alun should have seen this next move coming, but his hangover was too severe to contemplate anything that afternoon.

"Do we really need to see the caravan?" he asked, as he sat in his friend's passenger seat.

"A little peak won't hurt," said Rhiannon, tapping away on her steering wheel to the sound of "The Day We Caught The Train" by Ocean Colour Scene. She had listened to enough Ed Sheeran for one Christmas and was back in control of her music again.

Alun was less jovial. He knew full well what taking "a little peek" meant, and it usually involved breaking and entering. His raging headache was enough to put him off Christmas again for life. All that festive cheer was very exhausting, and it seemed to only cause upset and despair in the long run (or it certainly had for young George).

As always, he had decided, it was about *balance*.

"Did you want to pop by the station on the way?" asked Alun, as they entered Llanlyn.

Rhiannon saw the twinkle in his eye and knew what he was

thinking. "Alright," she said. "If we must. I'm sure the gift shop has plenty of new toys for you to look at."

"I don't know what you mean."

"Sure, sure. You know, if you'd prefer to just join their team of volunteers, I'm sure they've got a spare pair of dirty overalls."

Alun knew better than to indulge her with a response. Instead, he relished the thought of a new addition to his little, private world.

They pulled into the station car park to find two figures arguing in the distance. It became apparent, once they had left the vehicle, that these two individuals were Reese and Twm, the younger members of the station's volunteers.

Reese seemed to be the one in control of this heated exchange and continued to hurl a tirade of verbal abuse towards his larger, and yet, more timid counterpart.

Reese finished his rant by storming off, and he left the gentle giant to wallow in a pool of self-pity.

"Never a dull moment," said Rhiannon, as she lead her partner in crime through the main gate.

The two parted ways as soon as they approached the platform, one opting for a quick coffee from the café and the other preparing to satisfy his newfound appetite for miniature locomotives.

Alun entered the gift shop with the confidence of a returning local hero. Their number-one-customer was back, but, as he looked towards the counter, the accountant was surprised to find someone very unexpected manning the fort.

"Oh," he said. "I was expecting to see Lowri."

Roger Plewes, previously seen conducting the train, was now restocking one of the shelves. "Lowri's off sick today," he said, rummaging among the boxes and looking very stressed.

"But who's conducting the train?" Alun asked.

His question only seemed to upset the frazzled man even more. "Mr Simon."

"The station master?"

"Uh, yes. He said my skills are better off utilised somewhere else for the time being." It still pained Roger to even utter those words, and he did his best to pull himself together. "So he relocated me here to assist with Lowri in the gift shop."

Alun could see the man's crushed spirit, and he didn't want to pry any more than he already had. He headed straight over to his favourite shelf and began salivating over a replica fire station. As much as the man was in heaven, it was hard to fully enjoy himself with the banging noises on the other side of the shop.

"This blasted thing!" Roger cried, banging his label gun against the side of a box.

"Is everything alright?" asked Alun who had been forced to tear himself away from all the temptation.

"It's got stuck again," said the conductor-turned-shop assistant. "Look at me — I can't even be trusted to label up some boxes!"

He threw the label gun away and began sobbing into his hands. Alun stood there beside him, struggling, as he always did in this situation.

"They're going to toss me on the scrapheap," said Roger with a sniffle of his nose. "I'll be just like one of those old trains out there in the yard. I'll never be allowed to work in the railway industry again when they find out."

"When they find what out?" asked Alun.

The man looked up at him through his fogged-up glasses. He seemed reluctant to admit what he was about to say: "Someone's taken money out of the till," he said, pointing towards the counter. "I've been trying to work out what I'm going to do. I've counted it all six times now, and there's almost half of it missing."

Alun looked over at the till. "Have there been many people in here today?"

"Enough," said Roger. "Mr Simon will be fuming. I was only supposed to be in charge for one day. They'll probably even suspect me of taking it. But I didn't, I swear!"

The distraught man's face pleaded with his customer. Alun believed him but could see his predicament. "Did you leave the shop unattended at any point?"

Alun's question only seemed to worry Roger even more. "Only to use the loo! When you get to my age, you tend to go more often."

The accountant gave him a grave nod. An opportunistic thief only needed a few seconds to make their move, and it sounded like they had more time than that on this occasion.

Roger stared at the pile of boxes he had yet to put on the shelf. It stood there, taunting him, like a symbol of his incompetence. "I used to be a valued employee," he said. "Thirty years I worked in that ticket booth. Then I got pushed out by a flaming computer."

"How did you end up working there?" asked Alun.

Roger shrugged. "I've just always loved trains, ever since I was a small boy. I was never mechanically-minded enough to become an engineer, but I knew there were other jobs I could do. I would have done anything to work in that industry, anything to be involved. Then a position came up and that was it. It's all I ever wanted."

Alun smiled. He understood the fascination well. It had taken him a lifetime before he was reminded of his own interest in this historic method of transport. "At least you're still surrounded by trains," he said, pointing to all the merchandise around them.

"Not for long," Roger muttered with a heavy head.

"How much has been taken?"

"About three hundred pounds…"

Alun removed his hand from his wallet. Despite his charitable mood, even *he* couldn't come up with that amount of physical cash in time.

"Well," he said. "You never know, it might turn up somewhere. Could just be a misunderstanding."

The former conductor humoured him with a nod.

Over in the café next door, Rhiannon was waiting for her cappuccino to arrive. Gasping for a cup of hot, frothy goodness, she was surprised to be presented with a mug of strong instant coffee.

"Sorry," she said, "but I asked for a cappuccino."

Nerys Haf towered over her table with a cold stare. "Cappuccino's a coffee. That's a coffee."

Rhiannon looked down at the undissolved clumps of coffee granules floating on the surface. "Mmmh… technically a cappuccino has heated, frothy milk. But anyway…"

"We don't do frothy milk."

Her disgruntled customer glanced over at the steamer on the other side of the counter. "Then what do you use that for?"

Nerys took notice of the machine as though she hadn't even seen it before. "It's broken."

Rhiannon sighed and was left to enjoy her cold drink in peace.

The door swung open and Reese marched in with his stained overalls. The reluctant volunteer (as he was so fondly nicknamed around the station) headed to the counter and grabbed himself a *Mars* bar.

"Put me down for one of these, Nerys!" he called.

The café attendant appeared quicker than a supernatural being. "We don't put anyone down for anything in here. You can pay for it just like everyone else."

"Come on," said Reese. "I'm starving! I've not got any cash on me. I'll bring it tomorrow."

"Then you can eat your *Mars* bar tomorrow."

The young man was about to throw a hissy fit, when he was handed some coins.

"It's alright," said Rhiannon. "This one's on me."

Nerys reluctantly took the change and made sure to count it, thoroughly.

"Oh, thanks — you're a legend!"

Reese took a seat and began devouring his snack with the conviction of a hungry animal.

Rhiannon dragged her own chair over and sat beside him.

"It won't help you in the long run," she said. "You'd be far better with a banana."

"A banana?" Reese snarled to reveal his chocolate-covered teeth. "Where's the fun in that?"

Rhiannon gave it some thought. "You've got me there."

"Look," said Reese, after swallowing the last of his sugar fix, "I appreciate the *Mars* bar, like, but I'm not looking for no health advice."

"I'm the last person who should be offering any of that," said Rhiannon. She watched him licking his fingers. "Plus, I can see you're doing perfectly fine on your own." The man nodded and seemed to agree. "So, I hear you've had trouble getting work."

Reese scoffed. "Why else do you think I'm here? I've never worked with so many clowns in my life." He scrunched up his wrapper and gave her a suspicious frown. "Why? You offering me a job or something?"

"I'm afraid I don't have that kind of power," Rhiannon replied.

"So who told you about my work situation?" Reese's suspicions were growing rapidly. He had been so hungry for a snack bar that he'd failed to stop and question this stranger's unusual act of generosity. Now he was fully engaged and sniffing her out like an apprehensive canine. There was no such thing as a free lunch — or, indeed, a free *Mars* bar.

"I think it's fair to say that your bumpy history with the law is common knowledge around here."

"I've been inside," said Reese. "That's no secret. I ain't ashamed of it. But it doesn't make me a criminal."

"I never said you were a criminal," said Rhiannon. "It's admirable that you're trying to get back into the workforce with such a disadvantage. It can't have been easy."

Her compliment seemed to ease the man's paranoia, and he sat back in his chair with a newfound feeling of self-pity. "People have no idea. A record is a record in the eyes of an employer. You make one mistake and you're prejudged for life. They have these programs for newly released offenders to help find work. But you barely get a look-in for a job shovelling cow manure. I'm not a flaming axe murderer! There's weirder people around this station than there were inside."

"What do you mean by that?"

Reese folded up his arms and realised he was oversharing. "Oh, nothing. I'm just surrounded by idiots. I'm better than this place. I should be working for money — not free biscuits."

"You get free biscuits?" Rhiannon could hear her stomach rumbling.

"Nah. Nerys always says she never has any left."

The journalist looked over at the café worker with her steely gaze. "That doesn't surprise me." She took a big gulp of her drink, having forgotten about the dreadful taste. She scrunched up her nose in disgust. "How do you get on with your young counterpart?"

"Hey?"

"I think his name's Twm."

"Oh..." Now he knew exactly who she was referring to. "Like

I said, they'll let anyone work here. The guy causes more problems than he fixes. I don't really bother talking to him much."

"You seemed to be having a good old chin-wag when I arrived earlier," Rhiannon said, waiting for the desired reaction. It came quickly, and the man shot her a furious scowl. "We could see from the car park. It looked quite intense."

"It was no big deal. Twm was just being stupid again, as usual. He's a walking accident waiting to happen. No regard for health and safety."

"I thought you weren't big on health?" Rhiannon gave him a smug grin, and he stormed off without saying a word. The journalist felt a shadow moving across her, and she turned around to find Nerys standing there.

"Have you finished with that?" asked the café attendant.

Rhiannon looked down at her unappealing drink. "Uh, yes, I suppose —"

The woman snatched away the mug and returned to her little hole at the back of the room.

CHAPTER 22

Alun had told Roger that he could keep the change (not that there was any change left to give). At least the gift shop till was no longer empty, and he had secured the latest feature to his growing railway — its very own fire station. The excitement levels really were at an all time high.

As he walked along the platform with an extra skip in his step, the accountant couldn't help but notice a solitary figure sitting on the railway line.

"Twm!" Alun called out from the edge of the platform. "Are you okay?"

The young man was cross-legged in between the rails, and he looked up with a miserable expression.

"Nobody listens!" he called back. "Nobody cares!"

The concerned accountant looked around to see that the station was currently empty with not a soul in sight.

"I think it might be better if you get off the train track!" he called.

Twm shook his head. "I'm not leaving until the train gets here."

Alun checked his watch. He was quite certain that the young

man would be waiting a little while, as there wasn't another train for at least a couple of hours.

Mustering up all of the courage he could find, he stepped down off the platform and seated himself next to the volunteer.

"What are you doing?" asked Twm.

"I just thought I'd join you," said Alun. "It's hard to hear from all the way over there."

"But — there's a train coming. You'll be *squashed!*"

Alun double-checked his watch again. "I'll move in a bit."

This unexpected turn of events seemed to distress Twm even more, and he didn't quite know what to do with himself.

"Has this got anything to do with your argument with Reese?" asked Alun.

Twm went back to his dark mood and hunched over with his giant shoulders. "I hate him."

"I'm getting that impression."

"He's always bossing me around all the time — and he's not my boss! He thinks he knows everything. I've been here longer than he has, but he treats me like I'm stupid!"

Alun could feel his own backside start to go numb against the freezing-cold sleeper and began to doubt his chosen strategy. "What was he so cross about?"

Twm curled up even more, until he was huddled together like a humongous ball. "I told him I know about the stealing."

"*Stealing?*"

"Roger asked us about some missing money, and I saw Reese go into the gift shop — he never goes into the gift shop! So, I asked him what he was doing in there..." He sniffled and wiped down his wet nose. It was hard to tell whether it was the pent-up emotions causing him to sob or the freezing conditions. "He went mental at me — said it was none of my business — but I know he took the money!"

"How can you be so sure?"

"Because he used to steal my lunch!" The sobbing deepened and tears began to trickle down his cheeks. "That was my lunch! *Mine!* And he took it. I even saw him eat it."

"Did you confront him about it?"

"He used to just lie. He always lies! To everybody! He told me it was his lunch and to stop being such a baby." The tears of sadness very quickly morphed into tears of rage, and his face went red, as he clenched his huge fists. "He makes me so angry!"

Alun could feel the man's body temperature rising and began to get a little worried about his own safety. It was clear that Twm was not a person who had an awareness of his own strength, and the accountant did not fancy being the result of any collateral damage.

"Did you tell anyone else about him?" he asked.

Twm shook his head. "Nobody ever believes me anyway. And Reese said, if I tell in him, he'd —"

Judging by the volunteer's second burst of sobs, Alun did not need to hear the rest of the sentence. He got the message. "I believe you," he said.

Twm went quiet and turned to him with a confused stare. "You *do*?"

"You've got no reason to lie. And I'm sure Reese's behaviour will catch up with him in the end."

Alun had no idea if what he was saying had any truth, but it seemed to make Twm feel better. The two of them smiled, and just before either of the two men could say anything further, they were startled by a furious cry: "What do you think you're doing?!"

They looked up to see Rhiannon standing on the edge of the platform with her hands on her hips. "Uh, we were just —"

"Get over here *now!*" she cried. "Before I come down there! Do you know how dangerous that is?!"

A terrified Twm hurried to his feet and went running back

onto the platform. Alun watched him in complete awe. Had it only been that persuasive, he thought.

"Now!!" Rhiannon roared and sent her panicked friend running off the track. "Honestly," she said, once everyone was safe. "I leave you alone for two seconds..."

Alun was about to explain what had just happened but realised that there was little point. He could barely understand why he had chosen to sit on the railway line himself and decided to put it all down to a moment of pure madness. These moments often occurred during times of high stress, and this Christmas had been very stressful indeed.

He turned around to find that Twm had already disappeared. The man moved very quickly for a person of his size, he thought.

"Are you ready, then?" Rhiannon asked.

Alun saw that same familiar, adventurous glow in her eyes, and he didn't like it one bit. For he knew what was about to come next.

CHAPTER 23

"I still don't think this is a good idea."

Alun had issued his warning for the seventh time that day, and it hadn't seemed to make much difference. They entered the field and made the short walk to the old, abandoned caravan. The houses of Llanlyn could be seen on the other side of the stone wall which ran along one side of this small patch of land. The grass was in very poor condition, and it wasn't difficult to see why the previous tenant of this field had been allowed to stay.

Rhiannon headed straight for the caravan door and was surprised to be met with little resistance. "The lock's broken," she said, swinging the door open.

"Maybe it was the police," said Alun. "I'm sure they would have been quick to search the place."

They peered inside at the modest home which seemed to have been ransacked by a pack of wolves.

"Whoever it was," said Rhiannon, as she climbed aboard with a single leap, "they could have had the decency to clean up after themselves."

Alun joined her inside and was struck by the damp smell. "I

can't imagine two people living in here," he said, sitting himself down on the narrow sofa.

"I think it's quite romantic, isn't it?" Rhiannon sat on the opposite side of the flimsy table crowded with personal possessions. "Two people, living on their own terms, moving around like free souls."

Alun sat back and tried to imagine such a life. "But what are you supposed to put down for a billing address?"

His friend shook her head in disgust. Trust *him* to worry about the administration, she thought.

"I just think I prefer my home without four wheels," Alun continued. "I've never liked the thought of moving house."

"Really? You've never been tempted to take a one-way flight to Jamaica and sail around the Caribbean?"

The accountant shook his head. "I get sea sick."

Rhiannon was reluctant to respond and noticed her hand was resting on a jewellery magazine. "Looks like Hefin had some quite expensive taste for a man living in a caravan."

"Maybe he was looking to pawn something off," said Alun. "It can't have been easy not having a form of income. Unless he had a pension."

"Hefin Charles and his wife don't seem like the pension-kind-of-people."

"They must have had *some* money put away."

Rhiannon looked around at the messy caravan. "Wherever it is, I doubt it's in here."

After spending the next half an hour rooting through clothes, books and other various accumulated possessions, they came across a large photo album stashed away in one of the overhead cupboards. The dusty book landed against the fold-out table with a heavy thud.

"You can't beat physical photos," said Alun, flicking through the pages.

"Most of my family snaps are all on my phone."

"Really? What happens if you lose that?"

Rhiannon pointed upwards towards the ceiling. "The cloud."

Ah, yes, Alun thought. He'd heard all about "the cloud". Ffion had been discussing this with him only the other week, about migrating all of his paperwork to "the cloud". He was all for helping the environment, but there was nothing like the feeling of a physical ledger in your hands.

The faces of Hefin Charles and his wife whizzed by like a sentimental slideshow. A stream of memories had been immortalised for the world to see, and it was clear that the couple had been very happy in their life of simplicity.

"Doesn't something strike you as odd?" Rhiannon asked.

Alun paused before his next page turn. Normally, he was the one who spotted unusual anomalies. "What do you mean?" he asked.

Rhiannon grabbed the book and did a giant flick-through. The pages moved so fast that it seemed to animate the two smiling faces. "These all seem quite recent. There doesn't seem to be anything from their past lives — you know, before they started living in a caravan."

She wasn't wrong, Alun thought. "Maybe they wanted to start from scratch." He caught a flash of something as she turned the pages. "Wait! What about this one?" The accountant placed a finger on the page in question and turned her attention to a black and white photograph with two young men and a young woman.

"Wow," said Rhiannon. "This is a big time-jump. When do you think this was taken?"

Alun pulled out the photograph from its transparent seal and studied the faces. "It was a very long time ago," he said. "I'm assuming that two of them are a young Hefin and his wife. But they look barely in their early twenties."

Rhiannon stared at the other face. "I wonder who this gentleman is?" She watched Alun flip the photograph over to reveal a handwritten message on the back: *Eddie, Pennies From Heaven. All my love, Jimmy X*

"I'm guessing Jimmy?" asked Alun. "And who's *Eddie*?"

"What's that?" asked Rhiannon, pointing to a folded-up piece of newspaper shoved into the corner of the plastic covering. She pulled it out and revealed a faded newspaper article from the nineteen-sixties. The headline read: *£8 Million Hay Hill Heist*

Alun's eyes widened at the large figure. "That's a lot of money."

Rhiannon skimmed the first few paragraphs. "Hay Hill's in central London. This must have been a huge story at the time. I doubt this has been taken from *The Merioneth Press*."

"I've never heard of the Hay Hill Heist. But I'm no expert on famous robberies."

As the two trespassers continued their search of the lonely caravan, a silent figure was watching from the other side of the field. This person had been following their movements from the moment they had first entered the gate, and they continued to wait, patiently, until the two people had re-emerged into the fresh air. Little did Alun and Rhiannon know it then, but they were about to be confronted by someone very unexpected.

CHAPTER 24

Alun and Rhiannon leapt back in terror, as they looked down at a pair of snarling jaws.

"Lily! Stop it!"

The Miniature Schnauzer obeyed her master and let out a final bark of protest.

Lowri Medwyn stroked the dog's head and turned to address the two people standing on the other side of the gate. "I'm so sorry," she said. "She's been very grumpy today."

Rhiannon was still in two minds about opening the gate and decided to hold off.

"I thought you were on holiday," said Alun.

Lowri smiled. "A holiday would be lovely. No, I always take this day off every year." A sadness washed over her. "It's my wedding anniversary."

The other two both looked at each other. Her expression implied that it was not necessarily a happy occasion.

"My husband's been gone for over ten years now," said Lowri. "But I still like to celebrate in my own way."

"I'm sorry to hear that," said Alun.

"Oh, don't be silly. It's not like it happened recently.

Although it still feels like that sometimes. We used to do a daily walk together around this village. I've tried to keep it up ever since. It's nice when a place reminds you of someone."

Her gaze landed on the caravan over in the distance, and the other two noticed.

"I assume you probably know who that belongs to," said Rhiannon, pointing to the mobile home.

Lowri nodded. "I pass it every day and keep thinking he's going to walk out through that door." She shook her head in dismay. "When you get to my age, the people around you start dropping like flies."

Alun could certainly sympathise with the feeling of people dropping like flies. Over the last year, since Rhiannon had first knocked on his office door, he had never known so many people to drop dead in such a short space of time.

"You're probably wondering why we were in there," he said.

Lowri raised an eyebrow. "Do I *want* to know why you were in there?"

"Probably not," said Rhiannon. "But we thought Hefin wouldn't mind, especially if it might help catch his killer."

The gift shop volunteer let out a cold shudder. "You both must be freezing," she said. "Do you fancy popping round mine for some mulled wine?"

Alun and Rhiannon were more than happy to accept her offer, especially if there were hot drinks involved. Lowri's bungalow was less than five minutes walk away from the caravan, and it wasn't long before they relocated to a more cosy environment.

"We shared a lot in common," said Lowri, as she placed down a tray of mince pies for her grateful guests. "We were both widowed, of course, but it wasn't just that. You know that feeling you have when you make a true connection with someone? Like you were destined to be good friends?"

"I have an idea," said Alun, who received a curious glance from the person sitting next to him.

"Is that right?" Rhiannon asked.

The accountant paused. "Why, yes. My dog, Peg, remember? It's like we were supposed to find each other."

"Oh, right. Yeah, of course..."

"Hefin had such a kind heart," Lowri continued. "He loved helping people. And he loved his community."

"Did everyone in the community love him?" asked Rhiannon. "After all, he didn't exactly pay council tax."

The accountant was rather surprised to hear his friend talking about council tax — or any tax for that matter. It was normally him that was interested in matters relating to HMRC.

"Everybody loved having him around," said Lowri. "His wife was also a wonderful person. The poor dear."

"Is it right that she died of cancer?" Rhiannon suddenly felt bad for having half of her mouth full of pastry whilst asking such a question. It was a hard swallow.

"Yes," replied Lowri. "Sadly. It's such a horrible disease. People are taken far too young."

"I don't want to sound insensitive," said the journalist, "but is there anyone you can think of in this village — or anyone at the station — who wanted Hefin Charles dead?"

Lowri took a moment to process the question, as though it was a subject she had given much thought about. "I've been racking my brains for days. I know practically everyone in this village — or, at least, I *thought* I knew them. I can't even think of anyone who would own a gun, let alone use it to shoot someone.

Alun studied her eyes. Human psychology had never been his strong point, but even he could tell that this woman was hiding something. "You said that you've been thinking about it a lot," he said. "What makes you think it was even someone from this village?"

The woman sighed and shook her head. "I don't know. There was something about his behaviour over the last few months. He seemed almost paranoid."

"In what way?" asked Rhiannon.

"He started talking about everything differently, as though he didn't feel he was long for this world. As though he knew his death was coming somehow."

"Anything specific?"

"Well, at first I thought he was unwell. He even —" Lowri turned her back on them and rested her hands against the counter. "Goodness, I haven't told anybody this yet." Her two guests waited, patiently, for what she was about to say next. Instead of putting them out of their misery straight away, she reached into one of the drawers and pulled out an envelope. "Hefin gave me this the day before he died."

She handed Alun the envelope and let him pull out the handwritten note.

"He said," Lowri continued, "if anything were to happen to him, I was to open that envelope. I laughed at first, thinking he was joking. But he was very serious. I finally built up the courage to open it this morning, but, as you can see, it's all just a load of gibberish."

They all gathered around to read the three sentences scribbled down in black ink:

Some try to hide, some try to cheat; but time will show, we always will meet.

I am always travelling, have life, have sense but don't live.

I am in the beginning of the earth. I am at the end of the time. I appear two times in a week. I appear once in a year.

All my love, H.C.

"Sounds like he was quite the poet," said Rhiannon.

Alun was studying the note in great detail. "I don't think it's supposed to be a poem."

"I wouldn't know poetry if it hit me with a shovel," said Lowri. "It's not really my cup of tea."

"Shovel," the accountant muttered. "Mmmh."

The two women stared at him, waiting for the man to elaborate.

"Is there something you want to share with us?" asked Rhiannon.

Alun was snapped back into reality again. "Uh, no. Not yet, anyway. I'm just letting it sit with me."

His friend shook her head. She'd heard it all before. He was as cryptic as Hefin's note. "Oh," she said. "That's nice. Well, why don't you let it have a little sit down with you then. Tell it to take its time."

"Well," said Lowri, chucking her empty mug in the sink. "I certainly can't make no head nor tail of it all."

Alun re-read the lines again and smiled. "I think I might just know someone who might like to have a look at this."

CHAPTER 25

"They're all riddles."

George read through Hefin Charles' note with an eager twinkle in his eye.

"We said you'd like it," said Rhiannon. "Merry Christmas!"

She plonked herself down behind her work desk and let the intern bask in his new treat.

Alun was sitting in her spare chair, gazing around at *The Merioneth Press'* central hub. He never got tired of visiting the offices of a real newspaper, although it was always quieter than he would have expected. Perhaps it was another slow news day, he thought.

"You've probably already heard them," he said. "They're quite well known."

George nodded with a slight feeling of disappointment. He had hoped for a new challenge.

"Are you telling me you already know the answers?" asked Rhiannon, turning to the accountant.

"They're quite famous," said Alun.

The journalist scoffed. "Famous? With who? Little hobbits who live in caves?"

"Do you really not know the answers?"

"No! Because I'm not hanging around in student unions playing *Dungeons And Dragons!*" There was an awkward pause. "Well, come on then — are either of you going to tell me the answers, or not?"

The two men looked at each other and shrugged.

"The first one's *death*," said George. "Some try to hide, some try to cheat; but time will show, we always will meet."

"I suppose it's quite obvious once you already know," Rhiannon muttered.

"Then the next one's the *Earth*," the intern continued. "I am always travelling, have life, have sense but don't live — the *Earth*."

"Obviously," said Rhiannon.

"And, then, the last one's the letter E. I am in the beginning of the earth. I am at the end of time. I appear two times in a week. I appear once in a year — the letter E."

"Great! So now we're back where we started: none the wiser."

Alun began muttering the answers to himself: "Death... Earth... Letter E..."

"Hefin's dead," said Rhiannon. "So there's the death. But he definitely wasn't living on planet Earth judging by that note."

"His name doesn't start with a E," said Alun.

Rhiannon sat up in her chair. "But his wife's name did. Her name was Emily."

"And she became a victim of death. Then there's the Earth..."

"What about earth — as in *soil*?" asked George.

"Yes!" his colleague cried out, making the man jump. "Buried in the *earth*. Like a grave."

"Why would he be referring to his wife's grave?" asked Alun. "And why tell Lowri?"

They all went silent and tried to make sense of this cryptic puzzle, seemingly left by a man who thought his days were numbered.

"Where is his wife's grave?" asked Rhiannon.

"It's in Llanlyn," said George. "I remember the funeral. Everybody went."

"Maybe he was just asking Lowri to make sure he was buried next to his wife?" asked Alun.

Rhiannon picked up the note. "Possible. But it's a strange way to ask. I mean, if you wanted to make a request like that, why make it so cryptic?"

None of them had the answer, and, eventually, George returned to his own desk to continue editing his latest batch of photos. As he scrolled through the images, the intern could sense a presence behind him.

"You got the Santa shot!" cried Morgan.

"Uh, yes." George turned to see his editor-in-chief peering over his shoulder. "We grabbed it on the way to the farm."

The editor gazed at a photograph of what appeared to be a very thin Father Christmas lying beside the railway line. He couldn't help but frown. "But... that's *you*, George."

The intern wondered who else his boss might have expected, but he didn't say anything.

"And I can see your face," Morgan added. "There's no beard."

"Uh, no. We didn't have enough left in the budget for a beard. So we had to improvise."

The editor took one last look and walked off.

On the other side of the room, Rhiannon was giving the intern a thumbs up. George lifted up his own thumb in return. The plan had worked.

Rhiannon had been adamant that they captured the worst possible looking photograph imaginable, and they had succeeded magnificently. No reputable newspaper would dare publish such an ethically questionable photograph, and, with the help of their terrible execution, the bad idea would hopefully remain exactly that: just a bad idea.

By the time Alun had returned back to Rhiannon's desk with a round of teas, the journalist was deep into an article about a nineteen-sixties diamond heist. The incident had intrigued her from the moment she had come across the newspaper clipping in Hefin's caravan, and it was about to intrigue her even more.

"Eight million," she said. "That was a lot of money back then. A lot of money now! Three of the gang members got caught, and one got away. The police only recovered less than half the goods." Her computer mouse froze. After scrolling further down the page, she was presented with three mugshots, one of which she recognised. "Alun, look at this..."

The accountant hovered behind her shoulder and glared at the screen in shock. He knew exactly what had caught her attention. Staring at him was the same face who had smiled at him earlier on in the caravan; it was the face of a criminal called Jimmy Rooney.

"That's the same man in Hefin's old photograph," he muttered. "Do you think Hefin was actually linked to the Hay Hill robbery?"

"I'd say he was more than linked," said Rhiannon. "I think he was probably the fourth member. The one who escaped." She read out the name of the fourth man: "Eddie Clark."

"Eddie..."

Alun held up the black and white photograph taken from the album and flipped it over. The handwritten note was still there: *Eddie, Pennies From Heaven. All my love, Jimmy X*

"Hefin Charles was actually Eddie Clark?" asked Alun "An *escaped diamond thief*?"

"It would make a lot of sense," said Rhiannon. "Travelling nomad, mysterious past, winds up in the middle of nowhere with his wife..."

"What about the diamonds?"

"Exactly. What *about* the diamonds? I'm sure that Jimmy Rooney is probably wondering that too."

Alun collapsed into the office chair opposite her and loosened his collar. It was very hot in the offices of *The Merioneth Press*, he thought. "You're not seriously suggesting that we're dealing with Jimmy Rooney — a diamond robber?"

Rhiannon wheeled her chair forwards so that only he could hear what she was about to say.

"Think about it: the hooded man with the shovel, the gun, the disturbed ground... I'm telling you — Jimmy "the diamond geezer" Rooney is hiding out in Llanlyn. He's probably out there right now, trying to find the diamonds."

Alun tried to imagine a notorious robber lurking in the shadows of Llanlyn station. It wasn't something he really wanted to think about, especially as he quite liked going to that station. He imagined a gruesome monster of a man with hollow eyes and a scar across his cheek. The whole idea made him shudder.

"Stuff like this just doesn't happen around here," he said.

"I'd say stranger things have probably happened," said Rhiannon, who couldn't help reflect back on the memory of a local woman who believed she was a witch. She rolled her way back to her computer. "But there's only one way to find out for sure if all this is true — and what a story if it is!"

Alun could sense what was coming, and he hoped that she wasn't about to say what he thought she was about to say.

"We need to find the diamonds before Jimmy does."

CHAPTER 26

Rhiannon was the last member of her team in the office that day. By the time six o'clock had rolled around, she was all alone, pouring over obscure articles on the Hay Hill Heist.

There was nothing that sold newspapers like a good-old-fashioned robbery, and she could see why. Seemingly victimless crimes were always easier to get behind, and it was hard not to root for people who stole from the super-rich in some elaborate heist that, on first glance, appeared to be impossible.

In reality, however, there was no such thing as a victimless crime, and someone always had to pay the price in the end. Whether it was the innocent employee of a London jewellers or the perpetrators themselves.

As Rhiannon began turning off all the lights before making her way out of the office, she wondered about Hefin Charles — or his alter ego, Eddie Clark — and whether he ever regretted his decision to commit a robbery.

A shower of falling raindrops was not something that Rhiannon had expected to face once she had reached the cold air outside, and the wait for the final alarm buzzer was a long one.

The tired journalist locked the front door and headed off down the narrow side street. Nightfall had already descended upon the small town, and it was only with the help of a pool of artificial light, coming down from a lonely streetlight, that Rhiannon noticed a figure walking away in the distance.

She would normally have thought nothing of it, only this particular person happened to be dressed in a hooded yellow raincoat.

"Hey!" she called out, wiping the rain from her eyes.

Her cry caused the stranger to immediately turn and run, an action that only further cemented the journalist's suspicions.

The yellow figure went running around the next corner, and, as the woman behind them cried out again, they sprinted down a second alleyway. Puddles splashed across the pavement, as the mysterious person went scrambling past Pengower's cherished pizzeria. Neon light from the restaurant's glowing sign created a trail of green ripples across the wet tarmac, as the hooded figure darted into a small courtyard at the back of the building and climbed straight over a brick wall.

Landing with a clumsy fall, the exhausted person dragged themselves over to an old van parked up against the nearby pavement. This hot and flustered individual leant against the bonnet to quickly catch their breath and was relieved to find nobody else around. They climbed into the driver seat and breathed an enormous sigh of relief, until the passenger door flew open to let in a burst of cold air.

Rhiannon climbed into the seat and shut the door behind her. "You're a slow runner, Hari."

Hari Malwen, Pengower's resident Santa Clause and part-time wheeler dealer, removed his yellow hood to reveal a red, sweaty face.

"How did you know it was me?" he asked.

Rhiannon folded up her arms. "Oh, I don't know... the red trousers... the gammy walk... the wheezy breathing..." She turned his attention to the ceiling. "Or maybe it was the giant reindeer sled fixed to the top of your roof?"

Hari cringed and nodded in defeat. "Fair enough."

"I suppose the question I *should* be asking you," asked Rhiannon, "is why you've been following me all this time?"

"Who says that I have?"

Rhiannon groaned. "Come on, Hari. You've been spotted more times than a house sparrow. That yellow raincoat is hardly inconspicuous."

"I've no idea what you're talking about."

"No? Then why don't I ask the police why you were spotted near Hefin's body?"

The man twisted his head to the side and glared at her in horror. "Spotted by who?"

"By a very reliable witness with a pair of long range binoculars."

Hari went from shock to outrage. "I had nothing to do with that murder!" he roared.

"And you know what? I think I believe you, Hari. But the police might not once they start investigating you. Doesn't look good, does it? One Santa knocking off another Santa before taking their place. Would make a great news story, though."

Raindrops patted against the windscreen, as the glass began to steam up from their warm breaths.

"Listen," said Hari. "That Hefin Charles fella was the one who came to me first. Alright? I barely knew him."

"What did he come to *you* for?"

"He got in touch a couple of months ago. I live up on the estate in Llanlyn, so he came round after being referred by a mate. Said he'd heard I was someone who was good at flogging things."

"Well, you told me that yourself."

"Yeah, and it's true. I love a good deal. And Hefin came to me with the deal of the century."

"Let me guess," said Rhiannon. "Diamonds?"

Hari seemed disappointed that she already knew. "He said he was desperate to get rid of them. Something about them holding a lot of bad memories that had come back to haunt him recently."

"Did he show them to you?"

The man shook his head. "Nah. Not that day. He showed me some examples in a magazine, asked if I was able to shift stuff that valuable off the grid. You know, without troubling *Her Majesty*. I assumed he was a bit of a tax dodger."

"You really assumed it was tax-related?"

Hari held up his hands like a foiled robber. "Hey," he said, "I don't ask no questions. It's none of my business what people get up to." He thought back to his meeting with Hefin and grinned. "I'll tell you what, it was a hell of a good deal. That ice of his was worth a fortune."

"Did you manage to sell it?"

"Didn't even get the chance. I asked to see the stuff, but he said he'd need to dig it up first. Then, a few days later, he called the whole thing off. Said he'd changed his mind and that his wife was going to keep it. But I know that's not true cause she's dead."

Rhiannon thought about Hefin's note. "And that was the end of it?"

"Aye, at least for a while. The morning he died, I got a call from Dyfed, the station master — right at the crack of dawn, he called. Dyfed lives in one of the cottages down near the railway crossing, see, and he'd run into his neighbour who'd just found the body. She was apparently in hysterics, and he helped her call the police. Dyfed asked if I could do the Santa gig that day at the station. Doesn't switch off, that guy. Typical military man."

Rhiannon was not surprised either. She had met the station's most senior member, and Dyfed seemed like the type of jobsworth to care more about his precious fundraiser than the death of a colleague.

"Anyway," Hari continued, "I asked about Hefin, and his neighbour had seen that the guy had been digging at the railway crossing. Dyfed reckoned he'd probably keeled over from a heart attack and banged his head. That was all I needed to hear..."

Rhiannon stared at him, the judgment pouring out of her like rainfall across the window. "You headed down there, didn't you?"

Hari shrugged. "I figured I was the third person in the world to find out about his death, and the clock was ticking. Hefin didn't need the diamonds anymore, so I would have been an idiot to just leave them buried in the ground."

"Idiot's a good word."

"I headed straight to the crossing, as fast as I could, with my own shovel. Once I found Hefin's body, I knew it weren't no heart attack that had killed him. Someone had done a hit on him. So I scarpered before the pigs got there."

Rhiannon stared in disgust. Hari was a true scavenger, she thought. "Why were you following us on the day we were there?"

"I weren't following," said Hari. "Ever since the old bill cleared off, I've been popping down to that crossing quite regularly to have a rummage. Figured Hefin might have forgotten where he'd buried the diamonds and that they were still out there somewhere. Worth a try. There's always a chance. That day I found you lot poking around. I've been curious about what you were looking for ever since."

Rhiannon slowly digested the new information about Hari's involvement and realised that she was no closer to solving this great mystery than Hari Malwen.

"I'm sorry to disappoint you," she said. "But, so far, I've found a whole lot of nothing."

"That makes two of us then!" The man let out a croaky laugh which wasn't reciprocated.

His passenger opened her door. "Goodnight, Hari. Don't forget your ticket."

Hari heard the door slam and saw the soaking-wet parking ticket against his windscreen. The part-time Santa Clause let out a frustrated grunt and prepared to drive off.

CHAPTER 27

Alun placed the final piece into the great puzzle and sat back to admire his masterpiece. His creation was now complete. The little post office had been worth every penny, and his little world would have everything it needed. There was just one thing left: it was time for the great maiden voyage.

His little steam engine burst into life with a cheerful peep and made its first lap around the spare room.

Alun watched the fruits of his labour take on a life of his own, and he was struck with a feeling he had not expected: loneliness. He had hoped that the completion of his little railway project would have given him an overwhelming feeling of joy, but, instead, he was left with an emptiness that made his facial expression look as gormless as the ones on the tiny passengers lining his platform.

Listening to the hollow clattering noises of his tiny train, he had the strange urge to talk to someone.

"Hey," said the voice coming out of his phone, only a few minutes later. "What's up?"

"Nothing," said Alun. "Just thought I'd see how you are."

"Oh," said Rhiannon. "Fair enough. Well, I'm okay but Gwyl might have caught head lice from somewhere. I hope that's not what they are." The line went silent for a moment. "How's the Orient Express coming along?"

"It's finished."

"Thank God for that! How does it feel?"

Alun stared at the train, as it snaked its way around his spare room. "Not quite how I expected. Maybe it's not big enough." He heard a long groan.

"I think you need to find a new hobby."

"Like what?"

"I don't know. Golf, knitting, a musical instrument... that's what people normally do, right?"

Alun thought about it. "Does solving crimes count?"

"You have to actually *solve* some crimes first."

"Good point."

"I spoke to our friend Bad Santa earlier."

"Hari Malwen?" asked Alun. "What did *he* have to say?"

"Oh, you know, the usual nonsense. I think we can forget our theory about the person in yellow. Turns out Hari Vulture's been sticking his beak where it doesn't belong. He's the low-life that I took him for. It was strange seeing him away from the grotto. I barely recognised the bloke without his —"

Alun waited for her to complete the sentence but there was nothing but dead air. "Are you alright?" he asked.

"Oh, that's it..."

The accountant waited again. "What's it?"

"Something's just clicked. The beard! I think I might have nailed it."

It was normally Alun uttering a trail of broken sentences when he'd hit a eureka moment, and now the tables had turned on him. He finally knew what it felt like to be kept in the dark whilst someone was putting all the pieces together.

The sound of crisps crunching on the other end of the line almost pierced his eardrums.

"Are you still up for paying our respects to you-know-who tomorrow?" Rhiannon asked.

"Fancy catching the train?" Alun asked back. What he wanted to ask was — what exactly had his friend discovered that was so interesting? Unfortunately for him, he knew he would just have to wait.

CHAPTER 28

"I can't believe I missed it."

Alun stood on the tiny platform in disbelief.

"Not bad, eh?" asked Rhiannon, looking rather pleased with herself.

The accountant had prided himself on being quite an observant fellow, but this was an occasion he had been well and truly fooled. "So what do we do now?" he asked.

Rhiannon watched the steam train approaching, as it chugged its way towards the last stop of its journey. As always, Pengower was the end of the line. "We do exactly what we were planning to do today," she said.

Alun nodded before scratching his head. "And what is that, exactly?"

"We find the only piece of physical evidence left in this whole little caper," Rhiannon said. "The diamonds."

"It's not really evidence in relation to Hefin's murder, though."

"It's a cracking motive. And if Jimmy Rooney finds those diamonds before we do, he'll be long gone."

"You know what I'm about to suggest," said Alun with a frown, "don't you?"

"We'll tell the police when we find the diamonds," Rhiannon assured him. "Come on, don't you at least want a little peek at them? We're so close! Plus George can get a photo. Can't you, George?"

She looked around the platform and saw that her intern had disappeared. "George!!"

George was already halfway up a tree on the other side of the railway line. His colleague's cry almost caused him to fall to the ground, and he held his camera for dear life.

"George! Get back over here now! The train's here!"

Once Doris had rolled herself to a complete stop, the small train began puffing out steam with a chirpy whistle. Dyfed, the stationmaster (and interim conductor) came stomping out of the back carriage.

"How many tickets?" he asked, barely acknowledging the two passengers.

"Three," said Rhiannon. "Please."

Dyfed lowered his bushy eyebrows into a confused frown. He looked around the platform to make sure he wasn't losing his mind.

"Oh," said the journalist. "There's one more over there."

She pointed towards the tree with the struggling photographer. It was good enough for Dyfed, and he issued the tickets with a grunt.

"I didn't expect to see *you* doing this job, Station Master Simon."

The station master cringed at her remark. "Yes, well... if you want a job doing properly, you'd better do it yourself."

Rhiannon heard a sharp yelp, as her intern landed with a thud. "Couldn't agree more." She watched the man checking his watch. "You run quite a tight ship, I've noticed. Someone mentioned you're quite new to the role."

The station master was slightly flattered, and he stood up straight as though he was about to salute. "You have to maintain certain standards in a place like that, or it will descend into chaos."

Alun admired the man's philosophy — for he too was partial to a little order and structure in his line of work. Although something told him that the former military man was not talking about neatly arranged filing cabinets.

"Is it true you were in the army?" he asked.

Dyfed stared at him, suspiciously, and stroked his moustache. "Lieutenant Colonel. Welsh Guards. Where did you hear that?"

"I've been to the station quite a bit over the last week," said Alun. "I'm sure a few people have mentioned it."

Again, Dyfed was flattered that people took such interest in his military career, but, as much as he could have spoken about it for hours on end, he didn't have time for this idle chit-chat.

"All aboard!" he roared.

His two passengers jumped to attention and, soon, they were on their way. As the train made its return journey alongside Pengower Lake, its three paying-customers sat back and enjoyed the ride.

Santa's Grotto was back open for business over at Llanlyn Station, and the place was buzzing by the time they had arrived at their final destination.

Alun was the first to step out onto the busy platform, and he scanned through the crowd of festive punters in their winter coats. Through clusters of happy people, he picked out the familiar faces he had come to be fully acquainted with over his last few visits. They now stood out like a handful of glowworms, all dotted around the station, seemingly in the background.

Eben, the signalman was peering out from the safety of his signal box. Iestyn, the senior engineer, was tending to his train, avoiding eye contact at all costs with anyone who walked past. His two apprentices, Twm and Reese, stood nearby, watching all of the fun and laughter going on around them. Even Mr and Mrs Bowen from the railway line cottages were there that day, helping themselves to some homemade gingerbread cookies.

Rhiannon caught the eye of Hari Malwen, who was back in full costume before a line of eager children. She almost barged into frosty café worker, Nerys Haf, who, against her will, was back on cake-selling duties.

"Alun!" cried Lowri Medwyn. She was standing outside her gift shop whilst her new assistant, Roger Plewes, struggled on a ladder with an armful of Christmas lights.

The accountant wandered over with a smile.

"Did you want a quick browse?" asked Lowri, nodding her head towards the shop.

"Uh, no thank you. I think I've got everything I need now." Alun sheepishly glanced down at his feet. "Actually, I don't think model railway building was quite what I was looking for in the end. In fact, I'm thinking of learning the trumpet."

They both looked over at the brass band playing over in the corner.

"They could do with a new player," said Lowri, clearing out her sore ear. "So what brings you to Llanlyn today? Feeling Christmassy?"

Alun looked around to check that nobody was listening. "We're actually on a little treasure hunt," he said.

"Oh? How marvellous! Treasure hunts are fun."

"It's related to your note from Hefin."

"Oh..."

Alun checked again and lowered his voice. "We've solved the

riddles. I think Hefin wanted to leave you something, and we might be able to find it for you."

"Oh!" Lowri seemed overwhelmed but pleased with the news. "You really are a generous man, Alun. They should make you the next Father Christmas!"

The accountant visualised the dead Santa corpse lying beside the railway line and shuddered. "I might give that one a miss."

"Roger!" Lowri cried. "How are you doing up there?"

The frazzled man was still busy untangling his Christmas lights and appeared to have made them even worse. "Shouldn't be too long now!" he called from his ladder.

Over on the other side of the platform, George was observing the entire area through the comfort of his viewfinder. His lens scanned across the crowd of people like a voyeuristic security camera, and fired off a series of snapshots in a bid to capture the atmosphere.

"Hey!" a voice boomed.

The intern almost dropped his camera in fright, as a furious Station Master Dyfed Simon came marching over.

"Have you secured a permit for taking those?"

George stared at him as though he was speaking another language. "*Permit?*"

Meanwhile, Rhiannon was making the steep climb up towards the signal box. When she reached the top of the staircase, she took a long hard look at the busy platform. From up there, it was like witnessing another miniature model, only this one was bursting with life.

"You see all-sorts from up here," Rhiannon said, as she felt a presence behind her.

Eben, the signalman, stood in his doorway, and they both watched a mischievous child steal a handful of sweets from Hari's bucket of grotto treats.

"I think people forget I'm up here half the time," said Eben. "It's how I like it."

"I suppose it's what I would expect from a person who does all his talking in a darkened room." She turned around and saw him grinning in amusement. "You'll be pleased to know that you've gained a new listener. I'm officially a fan. Which reminds me — I'd like to make a request."

The DJ appeared intrigued. "Is that right? Be my guest."

"How about Pennies From Heaven?" Rhiannon asked. Her song choice surprised the man. "Is something wrong?"

"Uh, no. You just struck me as more of an Ed Sheeran fan."

"You're too kind."

"What's so special about *that* song?"

Rhiannon broke her eye contact and stared off into the distance. "I've been listening to it a lot recently. It's really growing on me." She saw Alun looking up at her from the platform and gave him a wave. "In fact, I think it's my new favourite song."

CHAPTER 29

The graveyard was no different to any other graveyard. Llanlyn Cemetery had everything a person could expect from such a location: gravestones, peace and tranquillity, personal tributes to locals from generations past. To the latest visitors entering the main gate, the site was hopefully going to contain the final answers to a mystery that might well have been decades in the making.

The last time Alun and Rhiannon were in a graveyard, it was under very different circumstances indeed. This time, there were no serial killing undertakers or deceased clairvoyants. Instead, they were at the tailend of a series of peculiar riddles, and there didn't appear to be another soul in sight (at least, not one from the land of the living).

They walked among the tombstones, searching for a name that began with the letter E. and whose husband would likely be laid to rest beside her very soon.

"There it is," said Alun, pointing to one of the more recent stones in the middle of the yard.

"That was quick," said Rhiannon.

The accountant was used to scanning through endless lines

of data, and the act of scouring through row after row of deceased names had been surprisingly no different.

George lifted up his camera and grabbed a quick snapshot. The name Emily Charles had been carved into the hard stone. Down below was a squared flower holder with the quote 'Pennies From Heaven' engraved against its marble-themed exterior.

Alun muttered the words aloud whilst Rhiannon crouched down against the long grass.

"Well," she said. "Here we are. Did anyone bring a shovel?"

Her companions looked horrified.

"Don't even joke about it," said Alun.

"What? Hefin's wife was probably cremated anyway."

"You don't honestly think that Hefin buried the diamonds in his wife's grave? That's worse than the idea of digging it up."

"I could grab a shovel from the shop," said George.

"No!" Alun cried. "There's no way we're digging anything up. Rhiannon was only joking. Isn't that right, Rhiannon?"

He turned to find her shrugging. "What were you expecting us to do here?" Rhiannon asked.

"I don't know. Certainly not that! I was hoping we'd find another clue."

"I think we've had more than enough of those. I'm not spending my time on a treasure hunt created by a guy who isn't even alive anymore."

Whilst Alun and Rhiannon continued to debate the ethics of daylight grave robbery, George had taken it upon himself to tidy up the dead flowers sticking out of their hole-covered grate. He tutted at the mess and, in the process of chucking away some crusty storks, the intern spotted something gleaming through one of the holes. After reaching down and removing the metallic grate from the top of the gravestone vase, George reached inside and pulled out a single diamond ring.

Alun and Rhiannon turned to him in disbelief. "Where did you find that?"

The intern pointed towards the solid box marked "Pennies From Heaven" and seemed to be rather pleased with himself.

They all gathered around the piece of jewellery and admired its large stone. Before any of them could say another word, the appearance of a pointed hand gun caused each person to gasp.

"Hand it over..."

George lifted up his quivering arm and handed over the ring like a reluctant hobbit.

The face of Roger Plewes let out an enormous grin and twirled the item in his fingers. "Now step away from the grave!" he roared.

Rhiannon and her gang did exactly as they were told. The man they had previously known as an eccentric conductor-turned-shop-assistant was now as cold as the December air. He had an air of confidence about him and a self-assurance that he would be getting exactly what he wanted.

"Jimmy Rooney. We finally meet. It was the beard and glasses that had us fooled. Who'd have thought a person could look so different after all those years."

Roger ignored Rhiannon's comments and remained fixated on the grave. "You!" he cried, pointing at the youngest member of the group. "Empty that thing onto the grass!"

George rushed over to the solid vase and gazed down through the open hole. "But there's nothing else in there! It's empty."

Roger (or Jimmy, as he had indeed been known for most of his life) lost his composure for a moment. "It can't be!" he roared. The more he spoke, the more it became apparent that his accent had a cockney twang. "Stop playing games, lad!"

"Is that really necessary?" Alun asked, gesturing towards the gun in his hand.

Apparently it was necessary, and Roger continued to wave his pointed barrel like a mad conductor (and not of the train-variety). "Check again!"

"Face it, Jimmy." Rhiannon stared him down. "The diamonds are gone. That's all there is."

"It can't be!" Roger's voice broke into a helpless whimper. "There must be more!"

"Is it really worth it?" the reporter asked. "All this for some old diamonds?"

The gun began waving around through the air. "It's not just about diamonds! I want my rightful share!"

"Is that why you killed Hefin — or Eddie, as you probably know him?"

Roger's lip began to quiver. "That was an accident."

"Really? Shooting someone and leaving them for dead was an accident?"

Alun was more concerned about another possible accident occurring, and he breathed a sigh of relief when the old criminal began lowering his weapon.

"He was my friend," said Roger. "If he hadn't been so stu —" The man wiped away his runny nose and tried to remain calm. "I spent twenty years of my life locked up without anything to show for it. Eddie was lucky. He was the one who got away. By the time the coppers had raided his flat, he was long gone. Eddie was always good at running away. But, this time, he took something that didn't belong to him."

"The stolen goods?" asked Alun.

"The love of my life." He went silent for a moment, as the others tried to take in what they had just heard. They all looked towards the gravestone.

"Pennies From Heaven," the man muttered with a longing smile. "That was her favourite song."

"Emily?" asked Rhiannon.

Roger dropped to his knees. "I didn't find out about her and Eddie until I got out. I had to hear it from Emily's mother. She said it was like the two of them had disappeared into a puff of smoke. They changed their identities and everything. By the time I tracked them down again, she was gone."

"It must have been quite a shock for Eddie when you turned up on his caravan doorstep," said Rhiannon. "Talk about a blast from the past."

"He had plenty of warning," said Roger. "When I found out they were living out here..." He looked around at the surrounding hills and mountains in the distance. "Living in this beautiful part of the world without any cares or worries... I started sending him little notes and keepsakes. He must have thought I was a ghost coming back to haunt him. And he was right. His reaction when I popped up working at the station one day was priceless." He let out a wicked smile. "I even found a nice little home for myself up on a local campsite, said I wanted a taste of this idyllic life of his. I'd been dreaming of it for years. I played it really cool, saying it was all water under the bridge. I wanted to make him sweat, and he did for months. After a while, I started to enjoy my new life as old bumbling Mr Roger Plewes, the incompetent conductor. It was the most fun I'd had in years. Even got quite close with that woman from the gift shop. Turned out Eddie had an eye for her too and that was perfect — you steal my woman, I steal yours."

Rhiannon rolled her eyes. She felt as though she was watching some old crime caper film where the men walked around like arrogant kings. Talk about a stereotype, she thought. "I don't want to hurt your ego," she said. "But I don't think Lowri Medwyn is really that into you. Call it intuition."

Roger shrugged. "It was all fun and games for a while. I was like one of those sea creatures, laying there in the sand, waiting for the right time to strike, right when their prey would least expect it. Trouble is, I got impatient. Eddie had run off with a load of the stolen goods, and he still owed me my share. I knew he still had them. You don't live in a caravan when you've cashed in a load of diamonds. The more time I spent here in Llanlyn, the more I realised that Eddie had changed. He wasn't the old crook I used to know. He'd mellowed. This life had made him soft. He was genuinely... happy." His face darkened. "That's when I decided to confront him one afternoon."

The other three listened, paying close attention to the lowered hand gun that still proved rather distracting.

"I rocked up to his caravan with a loaded gun," Roger continued. "I thought it would frighten the life out of him. But it was like he had been expecting it. The guy was even dressed in his Santa outfit after a morning at the grotto, and you can imagine how strange *that* was. I asked him what he'd done with the diamonds, and he said he'd buried them out on the railway line. We walked all the way out there. My arm was killing me after holding the gun for so long. Halfway there, he slipped on the ice and whacked his head. He was hurt, badly, but there was no way I was turning back. He started digging once we got to the crossing, but after an hour, I knew he was just stalling. When I offered to help, he came at me with the shovel. We wrestled on the ground for a bit and that's when the gun went off in my hand." A look of painful remorse swept across the man's face, as his eyes welled up. "He was my mate. I never meant to kill him. Even after everything he did, I just wanted my old friend back. We'd had some good times, me and him."

"Did you find the diamonds?" asked Rhiannon.

Roger scoffed. "You think I'd still be here if I had? I even carried on digging afterwards. But I found nothing. I decided to lie low for a while until the dust settles and the police lose interest. Then I'd go back there and dig that whole place up until I find them." He looked over towards Alun. "When I heard you tell Lowri earlier about some 'treasure hunt', I started to worry that you'd found something I'd missed. So I followed you over here."

"Well," said Rhiannon, "as you can see, we're no closer to finding any diamonds than you are. So if you don't mind, we'll head off now and leave you to it —"

"Don't move!" Roger hissed, his weapon now raised again. "You!" He pointed to George. "Go and fetch me a shovel!"

"You can't be serious," said Alun.

George pointed his barrel towards each one of them. "If you even think about calling the police, your friends are dead!"

The intern began walking, only to be stopped in his tracks.

"Wait!" Roger cried. "Give me your phone!"

"It's in my camera bag," said George.

"Hand it over!"

The young man pulled out his mobile phone and took a few steps forward. Just as he was close enough for his hand to touch Roger's, the camera in his other hand let off an enormous flash that caused the older man to shield his eyes. Having knocked off his own glasses, the short-sighted Roger was momentarily blinded, which was enough time for the others to flee for their lives.

By the time the flustered, old gangster had taken aim for his first shot, there was enough distance between him and his targets that they were safely out of range. With eyesight like his, he would have struggled to shoot an elephant in a field unless it was less than a few feet away. With a furious wail, he made his own escape towards the cemetery's back wall.

WITH HIS COVER BLOWN, Jimmy Rooney had walked as far away from Llanlyn as his legs would carry him. He had no doubt that the three people he had encountered in the graveyard would go straight to the police, and there was no chance in a million years he was going to go back inside.

Unfortunately for him, he had not expected to come across someone who was also armed. Little had he known it when crossing the last few fields, but the land he was traipsing over happened to belong to a farmer with a certain disdain for unknown trespassers.

"Drop your weapon!" Wali Henryd had cried from the safety of his hiding spot. "Drop it or I'll shoot!"

Frazzled by the call, Roger went spinning around and stumbled into the mud. They're after me already, he thought, and in a moment of sheer panic, he fired off his gun. What followed was an excruciating blow to his leg, as the farmer's response had resulted in another gunshot.

"You bloody fool!" the old robber cried, when he realised that his enemy was merely a trigger-happy farmer with a shotgun. "You shot me! You shot my leg!"

Watching the man wriggle in agony against the grass, Wali began to regret his extreme reaction and even felt a small degree of sympathy for the man. But the farmer reassured this stranger that he would do everything in his power to make it up to him, and he would even go as far as to nurse the man back to full health (once he had notified the police, of course). In the meantime, there was still plenty of time to share his theories on the great milk conspiracy. He was quite certain that a few hours of *that* would cheer the man up.

LLANLYN STATION HAD FINALLY CLOSED its doors for the day. Doris was tucked up in her engine room for the night, and the platform was now completely deserted. Apart from Eben the

signalman in his private box, not a creature was stirring —
except one.

In a quiet building, in the far corner of the train station, sat a
model railway. Gazing at this tiny world was a large figure.
Twm stared at the small lake in the centre of the model and
smiled. With his giant hand, he reached into the pool of stagnant water and pulled up a polythene bag which had been
weighted with a rock tied to a piece of string.

Inside the bag was a secret he had been sitting on ever since
Hefin Charles had sworn him to secrecy. Unlike all the other
volunteers, the old man had entrusted Twm, and the young man
would never let him down. He would make sure that his little
secret would never leave that very room, and whenever he felt
the desire to take a peek, he would have the freedom to do so.
Today was one of those days.

The objects inside the bag sparkled in the centre of his
pupils, as he emptied one of them into his hand. Resting in his
palm was the most beautiful thing he had ever seen: a diamond
the size of a small chestnut.

CHAPTER 30

"Oh, thank God! I thought you'd never get here!" Rhiannon pulled Alun inside the house by the scruff of his Christmas jumper.

The accountant was pretty certain that he had arrived exactly on time, but his nervous friend seemed to have lost all sense of time. The man had barely taken off his coat before she was pacing up and down her parent's foyer.

"Are you alright?" he asked, trying to hide the bag of Christmas presents in his hand. "You seem on edge."

"So would you be if you'd been trapped in a room with *that* lot for an hour," said Rhiannon.

"Oh, I'm sure it's not that bad."

"Alun!"

A slurring Morwenna Williams came lunging at him with a mouth stained with mulled wine. "Happy Christmas!" she cried, pulling him in for an overly long squeeze. "You made it!"

Rhiannon saw her friend's panicked eyes, as he was smothered in her mother's arms. He was starting to appreciate her previous complaint, and the journalist couldn't help but smile.

"Rhiannon!" Morwenna cried. "Fancy not giving our guest a proper welcome, loitering around here in the hallway. Come on, Alun!"

Her daughter looked on in despair, as her moment of pleasure became very short lived.

"Here he is!" Morwenna cried, escorting her guest into the living room.

Heads turned, and Alun felt a jolt in the pit of his stomach. He had never enjoyed being the centre of attention (not that it had come up very often).

Rhiannon's father, Trig, who had also started early on the mulled wine, came swanning over in his loud shirt. "Alun!" he boomed. "Good to see you, lad."

The accountant felt his hand buckle under the man's strong handshake. He felt Morwenna's arm hugging him tight and couldn't help but wonder whether it bothered her husband.

"Morwenna's been telling me a lot about you recently," said Trig. "Sounds like you're a busy man these days."

Alun quivered in front of him. "Oh, I wouldn't go that far."

"You calling me a liar?" There was a pause before the younger man realised he was being teased. Trig roared with laughter and patted him on the shoulder. "Don't look so terrified. It's Christmas!"

"How about you fetch the man a drink," Morwenna hissed at him. "Or is that too hard?"

Her husband shook his head and walked away.

"Let me introduce you to some people who are worth talking to." Morwenna led Alun across the room to the happy couple over on the sofa. "Awel, you remember Alun?"

Her youngest daughter looked up with a wave. "Course I do, mam! He was the same year as Rhiannon. Didn't you play on the rugby team, Alun?"

"Uh, no." The accountant hung his head. "You might be thinking of my friend, Arwel."

"Oh, yeah. That's right. How's he doing these days?"

"Not great," said Alun with a cough.

"Shame," said Awel. "I really liked him. Top bloke." Gregory let out an impatient cough. "Sorry, how rude! This is my new fiancé, Gregory."

Alun waited for the man to stand up, but he remained seated.

"Nice to meet you," said Gregory with a flap of his hand. "And what is it you do?"

"I'm an accountant."

"Really? Interesting. And how's that working out for you?"

"Uh, well, it's all I've ever done, I suppose."

"Alun has his very own practice here in Pengower," said Rhiannon, having appeared almost out of nowhere. She stood next to her friend, who was surprised at her sudden enthusiasm for his profession.

"Is that right?" Gregory asked. "A fellow business owner. You must feel very proud. I'm sure Pengower is the finance capital of Wales."

Awel gave him a playful nudge and they both chuckled.

"*Hughes & Sons* is the number-one accounting firm in the whole area," said Rhiannon. "Isn't that right, Alun?"

Alun hesitated with his nod. He wasn't quite sure where she had plucked *that* statistic out, but he supposed the word "area" was quite general.

"Well," said Awel, stroking her partner's shoulder. "Gregory's company produces television programmes."

"Reality-TV programmes," Rhiannon corrected her. She turned to Alun. "Specifically one called *Sloanies*."

The accountant tried to pretend like he knew exactly what she was talking about but was failing miserably. "Oh, right."

"You ever watch *Sloanies*?" asked Awel.

"It's alright," said Rhiannon. "It's okay to say that you've never heard of it. I don't watch it either. You'll only find it on one of those higher-numbered terrestrial channels." She could feel her sister's gnawing glare.

"What's that?" Gregory asked, pointing to the carrier bag in Alun's hand.

"Oh," said Alun. "It's just a couple of presents."

"Ooooooh!" Awel's enthusiastic noise alarmed the man greatly. "Presents for who?"

"Uh, well... one's for Gwyl. And the other's just a little one for Rhiannon."

Rhiannon lit up at the mention of her own name. "You got me a present?"

"It's just something small."

"Open it!" Gregory cried.

"Excuse me?" asked Alun.

"Yes," said Awel. "Open it!"

"We don't need to do that now," Rhiannon muttered.

"Open! Open! Open!"

The journalist gave in to the couple's irritating chants and began ripping open her present.

Alun felt his heart begin to race and began very quickly regretting his last-minute festive gesture. Rhiannon lifted up the velvet box.

"That looks fancy!" Awel cried.

They all stared in wonder, as a gleaming necklace was pulled out of its container. Rhiannon stared at it in disbelief. "You got me this for Christmas?"

Alun swallowed a hard gulp.

Awel and Gregory both looked at each other with awkward faces.

"That must have cost you a bomb," said Gregory. "Maybe Pengower really *is* the finance capital of the world!"

"Alun," said Rhiannon, caressing the sparkling stone at the centre of the pendant. "What were you thinking? It's too much..."

The accountant was lost for words. He wasn't quite sure what he had been thinking, either.

Their faces went a bright shade of red, and the couple on the sofa were enjoying every minute. After an uncomfortably long silence, Morwenna forced herself in between them and raised her glass.

"Isn't this nice," she said. "All of us together for Christmas!"

"Oh, yeah." Rhiannon cringed. "It's great."

"When we eating, Ma?" asked Gregory.

Morwenna's face turned sour. "My husband's sorting the food out today. Apparently my cooking's not good enough."

"I never said that," Trig called out from the doorway.

"You implied it," Morwenna called back.

"Cooking for this many people's not easy, love."

"How long's it going to be dad?" asked Awel.

"Well," said Trigg, checking his watch. "Let's see... shouldn't be long now. The delivery guy said he'd be here for half-past. But you know what these *Deliveroo* types are like — lazy bunch!"

The man saw both of his daughter's giggling into their hands.

"What?" he asked. "What's funny?"

His wife continued her cold stare. "You're unbelievable," she said and walked away.

ALUN AND RHIANNON both headed out of the dining room with full stomachs and dizzy heads. The meal had been quite eventful, especially after Morwenna had doused her husband's shirt with a glass full of mulled wine. The two friends had decided to sneak off before any more drama could unfold and found themselves a quiet alcove underneath the stairs.

"Thank God that's over," said Rhiannon. "That was the longest meal I've ever had."

"It was definitely memorable," said Alun.

"Gwyl really loved his present."

The accountant smiled and noticed that she was now wearing her necklace. "I thought he would. I used to love those things when I was his age."

"If he's not careful, he'll become an accountant when he's older."

"Is that such a bad thing?"

Rhiannon sipped on her mulled wine and thought about it. "Nah, I suppose not. Accountants are alright, I guess."

They shared a comfortable silence for a while before Rhiannon began playing with her necklace. "Thanks for coming," she said. "These family get togethers aren't easy. I feel a bit bad for dragging you here now."

"I quite enjoyed it, actually."

"Really?" She looked at his content face. "You really *are* a strange man."

"I'm starting to suspect that," said Alun, and they both chuckled.

"At least you're not still building model trains in your spare time any more."

"True. Although it's probably a safer hobby than solving murders."

"That's true." She rubbed her necklace again. "Thank you for the present, by the way. If you ever do something like that again, though, I might have to kill you."

Alun smiled. "I suppose people have killed for much less."

They both nodded in agreement. After another bout of silence, Alun couldn't help but notice something unusual.

"What?" asked Rhiannon. "What are you looking at?"

The accountant squinted. "Is that what I think it is?"

The journalist looked up to see a mistletoe dangling above them. "Yes," she said. "I think it is."

ABOUT THE AUTHOR

We hope you enjoyed this book. If you'd like to read more books in this new series, you can join the P. L. Handley e-mail newsletter and receive all the latest news on future releases.

Subscribe to the e-mailing list by visiting the official P. L. Handley website at: www.plhandley.com

Reviews are extremely important for new authors, so please feel free to leave a short review on the book's Amazon page. Doing so will be a huge support in helping to introduce other new readers to this book.

Stay tuned for Book Six in the Murder Ledger Mysteries.

Coming Soon...

Printed in Dunstable, United Kingdom